The
Monkey's
Wedding

The Monkey's Wedding

and other stories

Joan Aiken

*with Introductions from
Joan Aiken and Lizza Aiken*

Small Beer Press
Easthampton, MA

Small Beer Press
150 Pleasant Street #306
Easthampton, MA 01027
smallbeerpress.com
weightlessbooks.com
info@smallbeerpress.com

Distributed to the trade by Consortium.

Library of Congress Cataloging-in-Publication Data

Aiken, Joan, 1924-2004.
The monkey's wedding, and other stories / Joan Aiken. -- 1st ed.
    p. cm.
ISBN 978-1-931520-74-4 (alk. paper)
I. Title.
PR6051.I35M66 2011
823'.914--DC22
                                    2011004625
First edition 1 2 3 4 5 6 7 8 9

Text set in Centaur 12 pt.

This book was printed on recycled paper by Thomson-Shore in Dexter, MI.
Author photo © Rod Delroy.
Cover painting by Shelley Jackson (ineradicablestain.com).

Table of Contents

Introduction

Writing short stories has always been my favourite occupation ever since I was small, when I used to tell stories to my younger brother on walks we took through the Sussex woods and fields. At first I told him stories out of books we had in the house and then, running low on these, I began to invent, using the standard ingredients, witches, dragons, castles. Then doors began to open: in my mind, I realised that the stories could be enriched and improved by mixing in everyday situations, people catching trains, mending punctures in bicycle tyres, winning raffles, getting medicine from the doctor. Then I began mixing in dreams. I have always had wonderful dreams—not as good as those of my father Conrad Aiken, who was the best dreamer I ever met, but very striking and full of mystery and excitement. The first story I ever finished, written at age six or seven, was taken straight from a dream. It was called *Her Husband was a Demon.* And one of my full-length books, *Midnight is a Place*, was triggered off by a formidable dream about a carpet factory. Most of my short stories have some connection with a dream. When I wake I jot down the important element of the dream in a small notebook. Then weeks, months, even years may go by before I use it, but in the end a connection will be made with something that is happening now, and that sets off a story. It is rather like mixing flour and yeast and warm water. All three ingredients, on their own, will stay unchanged, but put them together and fermentation begins. A short story is not planned, in the way that a full-length novel is planned, episode by episode, with the end I sight; a short story is given, straight out of nowhere: suddenly two elements combine and the whole pattern is there, in the same way as, I imagine, painters get a vision of their pictures, before work starts. A short story, to me, always has a mysterious component, something that appears inexplicably from nowhere. Inexplicably, but inevitably; for if you check back through the pattern of the story, you can see that the groundwork has already been laid for it. The story of "The Monkey's Wedding," for example, was set in motion by a dream about an acerbic old lady hunting about her house for lost things and buried memories, combined with a news story about a valuable painting found abandoned in a barn; only after I had begun the story did I realise that the last ingredient was going to be a grandson she didn't even know she had lost.

Joan Aiken, 1995

The Making of a Storyteller

This collection of stories, some of which have never been published before, is taken mostly from Joan Aiken's earliest writing years in the 1950s and 1960s when she was working for the English short-story magazine, *Argosy*. They demonstrate her wide ranging stylistic ability, with subjects as diverse as a spinster castaway on an island of talking mice, a doctor's cure for a glamorous man-hating motorcycle stunt rider, a village that appears only for three days a year, or a vicar happily reincarnated as a devilish cat. All these ideas seem to pour out of an endless imagination, making bold use of eccentric and unexpected settings and characters, and at the same time demonstrating an evident delight in parodying a variety of literary styles from gothic to comedy, fantasy to folktales. But Joan always repudiated the suggestion that she was "a born storyteller." She would always argue furiously that writing was a craft, like oil painting or cabinetmaking, that she had learned, practiced, and developed over the years. She described this period of her life as a single-minded engagement with the writer's craft; and her grasp of the short-story form as the foundation of her literary career.

What is far from apparent from these wildly inventive and freewheeling tales is that this was in fact a bitterly difficult period of her life, when not long after the end of the Second World War she was left widowed and homeless with two young children. Having made the brave decision to try and support herself and her family by writing, she applied for a job at a popular short-story magazine. In many ways, as she often said subsequently, this period spent working at *Argosy* could not have been bettered, both as a wonderful distraction and consolation during a bad time, and as an unbeatable apprentice-ship in the craft of writing.

Joan's work on the magazine, as a very junior jack-of-all-trades, gave her a thorough editorial training while teaching her more than she had ever learned at school about the basics of grammar, punctua-tion, and spelling. Her chief task was to read dozens of stories from the hundreds of submissions that arrived in daily bales, and then to reply to the unsuccessful budding authors. She gave critical feedback and advice, while also learning a good deal in the process about what made a good story. Joan also met and interviewed for *Argosy* many of the successful authors of the time, talking to writers such as H. E. Bates, Paul Gallico, Ray Bradbury, and Geoffrey Household about their working methods. Finally, she was also able to supplement her fairly meager income by contributing all kinds of articles to the maga-zine: editorial pieces, poems, anthology features, and eventually, also the short stories she was starting to write herself. It was this fertile mix of potboilers and random pieces, rapidly invented space fillers, articles written to go with leftover illustrations, and cheerfully ironic com-mentaries on unusual news stories or eccentric scientific inventions, which really began to inform Joan's fiction and ignite her practically unstoppable powers of invention.

Under a variety of pen names, including the nicely tongue-in-cheek John Silver—a name stolen from the pirate in *Treasure Island*—Joan created some of her taller tales. Among these was a piece imagining, for example, the plot for a stage musical constructed entirely from the personal columns of a daily paper:

"Nick Lochinvar, a young Scot, is broke and broken-hearted. Owing to a revolution he has had to leave the independent Indian kingdom of Pawncore, where he was agent-general, and Kate, the girl he adored, who has stayed to look after the little prince, and taking only his pet mamba, Amanda. (Yes yes, we know you don't get mambas in India, but he had been in Africa first.) In a mood of black despair he turns to studying the psychology of donkeys. Finally, reduced to selling either his Scottish evening full-dress regalia or the faithful Amanda, he spots an advertisement for a snake-charming competition the prize for which, five thousand pounds, would allow him to restore his fortunes with Kate . . ."

—and much more, material enough for a sackful of stories. Suggested lyrics to the songs are included of course, for example "the tune that he croons in the rainy monsoon—'I've a bungalow deep in the jungle-o . . .'" which also pour out in the astonishing flow of her invention.

Joan imagined the publication of a simple 'First Reader' for the educational improvement of long-term prison inmates, with lines like:

"Has Dan got a hot rod?"
"No, but Ned can do a ton in his van. . . ."
"Run Jim run! I saw a cop pop out of the pub!"

Or she would create and describe entirely fictitious manuals, with names such as *Popular Errors Explained,* from which she would list an astonishing selection of 'quotations' from topics in the index— 'Crocodile, Death foreboded by sight of,' or 'Nine of Diamonds, the curse of Scotland,' or simply 'Absurd Notions, Universal . . .' All, of course, were invented to tickle the imagination of the reader, but at the same time such pieces were developing possibilities for mad plots in her own fiction.

This need for quick-fire creativity clearly fed Joan's fertile mind and produced endlessly zany plots, as can be seen from the subjects of the tall tales included in this collection—a sailor who brings home a mermaid in a bottle, the murderous nightmares of the advertising jingle writer. Every story is surprising in its premise but promises an even more extraordinary outcome, once you are acclimatized to the Aiken imagination.

Reading dozens of stories daily provided a perfect opportunity to study both what made appealing story content, and also what made a story memorable. Joan summed up the story-writing formula she worked out for the necessary combination of elements as "exotic background, touch of sex, twist ending, and a touch of humor if possible"—a formula that would enable her to sell as many stories as she could in order to keep the family afloat.

As well as learning to write fast and efficiently, Joan was also working to perfect her style. In her interview with H. E. Bates, she notes a remark of his that became one of her key precepts for short-story writing. She writes:

> "Besides inspiration and a lot of sheer hard labor, a story requires, for its germination, at least *two* separate ideas which, fusing together, begin to work and ferment and presently produce a plot."

Apart from scanning the small ads for inspiration, Joan always recommended keeping a notebook to record odd sights and overheard conversations, dreams and news items that would presently gel into a plot. She found that this moment of congruence often came, in her case, while she was dealing with household chores, although she noted wryly that "other writers like Coleridge took laudanum, Kipling sharpened pencils, or Turgenev sat with his feet in a bucket of hot water" while waiting for the inspiration to strike.

Beyond thoughts on plots, Joan records very definite principles on style, for example comparing the construction of a short story to that of a small fire:

> "You are trying to kindle the reader's interest, feeding it with little nourishing bits of fuel, not dumping on too much at once. Lots of people when they begin writing make the mistake of putting in too much description—describing is lovely—but the reader can only take so much at one time, and he will begin to skip."

Another basic piece of advice she gives is to "show things—don't just tell the reader about them. If your hero is stingy and selfish—or if the house where he lives is haunted—show it, show what happens" and this she carries out with relish. With true economy she will show her heroine ordering a length of rope long enough to hang herself, "staring straight in front of her like Boadicea" while the hero attempts to distract her from her apparently suicidal intention by telling a wild story of his own about the naming of his dog Raoul:

> "After the Vicomte de Bragelonne," panted Richard. "He was the son of Athos, you remember. He was jilted by Louise de la Vallière."
> "And has Raoul been jilted?" gasped Julia, much interested.

Show things she certainly does, while leaping from scene to scene with astonishing fluidity, garnishing the forward pace of the action with extravagant detail and often extraordinary dialogue, and evidently with no thought of restricting her self to the basic *two* necessary elements.

Describing one piece of early work she wrote:

"'This is too improbable,' an editor once said to me. 'I like this story but it is just too hard to swallow.' He was talking about the only story I ever wrote, flat, from real life, and it taught me a useful lesson about the risks of using unvarnished experience."

This must have been a turning point, as demonstrated by the wealth of wild improbabilities displayed in most of Joan's fiction from that time onward. Undaunted by years of struggle and relishing her hard-earned early success, selling these stories for twenty-five pounds a time, after many late night hours of honing, crafting, and rewriting, she certainly earned her reputation as a storyteller of wonderful skill.

Joan concludes:

"I suppose these lessons are the writer's next best reward after the act of writing itself, because they fill one with the impetus to start on another piece of work at once, and the resolve to avoid every pitfall and do it all much better this time."

Lizza Aiken, 2011

A Mermaid Too Many

It was always the same when George came home at the end of a voyage. As soon as the *Katharina* dropped anchor by the quay and the news spread through the town, Janet left whatever she was doing—today she was bathing the cat in the dish-tub—and rushed to buy the ingredients for George's favourite supper of shrimp-and-watercress soup followed by chitterling pie. That done, and after seeing that the whole house was as clean as a pin, which it always was, she put on the dark-blue Indian silk, the earrings George had brought her from Venice, and the Japanese slippers; then she strolled through a spray of the scent he'd found in Valparaiso, which was so potent that more than a dab of it brought all the males of the town howling round Janet's doorstep like timber wolves. Then she settled down to wait for George.

After supper they always sat on the sofa for a little, in front of the fire, and then George would get fidgety and say, "Let's go to bed, shall we?" And Sam the cat would be shut up in the kitchen—much to his rage, for while George was at sea, Sam slept on Janet's bed.

So it was this time. A gale was getting up, a dry gale; the little town rocked on its base, and the wind humping along the High Street made the cobbles heave, knocked the stars about in the sky, slammed windows and doors.

George swung up Harbour Lane with his duffel bag over his shoulder and Janet's present under the other arm. He was hungry, and

Joan Aiken

happy to be home after months of water and salt wind; his sealegs were still under him, and the narrow, walled lane pushed him from side to side like a ninepin. Next trip he was to have command of the *Katharina,* and he was in a hurry to tell Janet about it.

"You murdering sod!" he shouted happily at a cyclist who shot past, brakeless, down the hairpin alley. He hitched his heavy load to the left arm and went on up to Bell Cottage, pushing open the door with his knee.

"George!" Janet's arms were round him, and he noticed with pleasure the smoothness of the Indian silk, the scent of new-washed rush matting, Sam the cat sitting clean and furious by the fire, the weight and darkness of Janet's coiled hair, and the bowls ready on the table for shrimp-and-watercress soup.

"Lovely," he said, burying his nose and this time getting a tang of Valparaiso along with the shrimps and the matting.

After the first embrace they held away a little and scanned each other thirstily: Janet for any cuts or bruises that needed explaining or treatment, George to remind hnnself again of her beauty, which he had never forgotten, her beauty that held the warmth and darkness of wine.

Suddenly Janet's eyes fixed.

"What's that?"

"That's my present for you!" said George proudly, and he lifted it, with a bit of an effort, onto the mantelpiece: an outsize bottle containing a fullsize mermaid. At least she was a three-foot mermaid, and that's as large as they need to come.

George tipped the bottle in lifting it, and the mermaid sank to the bottom, but she slowly righted herself, levelled, and undulated from stem to stern.

"Her name's Emma. Isn't she lovely? Only one in the country, I shouldn't wonder." And George smacked the mermaid encouragingly on her bottle. She rotated slowly, over and over, then brought her face close to the glass and gazed at them, unwinking.

There was a silence in the room, and George, to fill it, said, "Pretty, isn't she?" again, and then, as the silence still went on, "How about the shrimp-and-watercress soup, Janet? I'm a hungry man, starving for your cooking, lass."

Janet nodded absently, went and came again with a bowlful of fragrant steam, and ladled the soup. It was plain her thoughts were elsewhere, and George had the unhappy feeling that the wine of her beauty had been corked up, so far as he was concerned. They ate without speaking, while Emma practised an end-to-end changeover with a double bend in the middle.

"Clever, isn't it?" said George. "She'll do that for hours, sometimes."

"Can she hear what you say?"

"I'm not sure," said George. "She isn't a one for talk. Sometimes she'll sing. I brought you the right food for her, dried seaweed." He got it out of his pack.

At this Janet's composure broke.

"You great gormless thing! Bringing that beady-eyed monster in here! You needn't think I'm going to sit on the sofa with her watching every move I make!"

"But Janet!" George was thunderstruck. "I brought her specially for you—she's your present."

"Well, I'm sorry, but she can't stay here."

"But last time I was home you said you wanted company—"

"Company! Not that sort of company." She pointed at Emma, who was blowing bubbles at them. "You'll have to take her back where she comes from."

"But damn it, Janet, that's the middle of the Mediterranean."

"Then sell her to a circus, museum, anything. I can't have her in this house another minute; you know I can't stand things in captivity, I'd never have a canary or a goldfish."

"Emma doesn't mind the bottle," he said. "She likes it, don't you, Em?"

Janet burst into tears. George tried to stroke and pacify her, but she ran upstairs and slammed the door.

"Not while that creature's in this house," she shouted through the keyhole.

Injured, crestfallen, George turned down the stairs again. There seemed nothing for it: Emma had to go. And perhaps it was as well, for Sam the cat had jumped onto the mantelpiece and was rubbing his loving length along the glass, through which Emma looked at him with malevolence.

Picking her up, George tramped heavily through the front door, put bottle and mermaid in the pram that stood in the porch, and moved off. A click told him that the door had been snecked against him.

Moonlight blew like silver dust in the empty street and on Emma in her bottle. George made his way to the Falcon, which was kept by Mrs Agnew, Janet's mother. Maybe she'd take Emma, and change the Falcon to the Mermaid. It was worth trying.

Mrs Agnew was in the saloon, small and grey, downy as an owl, beak and claws ready to strike.

"Well, George," she said, offering her cheek. "Home again. Captain next trip, I hear."

"Well, Mrs A., I brought you something from foreign parts." Mrs Agnew gave Emma one look and that was sufficient.

"Nothing of that kind in my bar, thank you, George. This has always been a respectable house and will remain so. I've no wish to attract *that* sort of custom."

"What shall I do with her then? said George miserably. "Janet won't have her in the house and I've got to find a home for her." He thought with longing of Janet's beautiful roundness under the blue silk, and of the creaks and twangs of the springs of her bed, and for the first time he began to dislike Emma, beady-eyed in her brine.

Mrs Agnew softened.

"There's Madame Lola from the fun fair. She's in the lounge this minute, talking to the captain. She might like a mermaid."

George picked up Emma and went through. Captain Beard and the fortune-teller were sitting in the leather-upholstered corner, very snug, talking about dreams.

"And it's a funny thing," said Madame Lola, "just lately, over and over again, I've been dreaming about plumbing. Big green baths, tiled pedestal basins—mains-flushes without those nasty cisterns—oh, beautiful it's been, Captain Beard. That's the trouble about a caravan like mine, I always say. You have a lot of conveniences, but you can't have what I call *superior* plumbing."

Captain Beard rumbled a laugh and tightened his arm, hawser-like, round her ostrich plumes. "You ought to come on board the *Katharina*," he said.

"Oo, should I? Why? I bet you've got some smashing plumbing there, Captain Beard, and you such a one for having everything just so."

Captain Beard rumbled again, thinking of slops and bilges. "Anyway I'm retiring," he said. "Going to live in the old house in Light-house Lane. Going to put in a bathroom and make it all shipshape. You'd better come and advise me about the plumbing, Madame Lola."

"Captain Beard! What ever will you suggest next? There, didn't I say I saw a devoted woman in your palm who was going to help you? Now, now, Captain, here's Mrs Agnew to tell us to behave ourselves."

But when Mrs Agnew asked her advice about Emma, Madame Lola had no suggestions to offer.

"I'm ever so sorry, but we reely couldn't have something like that at the fun fair. The R.S.P.C.A. are so particular, they'd be round my neck like a ton of bricks. Sorry not to oblige you, dearie."

"I told that boy he'd be courting trouble, taking a mermaid home," grunted the captain. "Overexcited, he was, getting his Master's Certificate. He'd have done better to leave that bottled nuisance where she belonged."

"Why not ask Mr Mack?" suggested Madame Lola. "He's so up-to-date since he's had the deep freeze put in, and all them climbing ivy plants in pots. He might like a mermaid for decoration."

So George took Emma over to Mr Mack the fishmonger, who sat browsing over the *Greyhound Dispatch* in another corner. Mr Mack lifted his shining bulbous eyes from the tiny folded square and had a good stare at Emma; then he said definitely, "No, my boy. Oh no. Whatever would my customers say? Why, it would be as good as making them think they was cannibals. Oh no, no, that wouldn't do at all. If I was you I'd give her to a zoo, yerss, that's what you want to do, give her to a zoo." And he flapped into his paper again.

"But there isn't any zoo nearer than fifty miles off," snarled George.

The lounge was nearly empty. Mrs Agnew was pointedly wiping the tiled tables and looking at her watch; Captain Beard and Madame Lola were seesawing towards the door, wreathed in one another's arms like a daisy chain.

"Why don't you ask the professor?" said Mrs Agnew over her tray of glasses. "The one that's staying with the old Miss Ruddocks? He'd know what to do with her, sure's you're born."

"Won't he be in bed by this time?"

"Never before two, not those old parties," said Mrs Agnew, gently shoving George out of the door. So he pushed the pram down through the moony wind to the big house on the quay where the Miss Ruddocks had lived since they came home from Turkey. At the first ring of the bell the older Miss Ruddock appeared behind the glass door like Cleopatra's Needle and graciously waved him into the morning room, where her sister and Professor Topole were drinking Madeira and watching the bobbing masts through the French window.

"He has a mermaid he wishes to dispose of," shouted Miss Ruddock above the wind.

"Can she speak Turkish?" asked Miss Laura, filling a glass for George. "We need somebody to converse with. Our Turkish is becoming sadly rusty. Or even Greek would be useful."

She fired some questions at Emma, but the mermaid had caught sight of her reflection in a Venetian mirror and paid not the slightest attention.

"I'm afraid she doesn't speak," apologized George. "She'll sing a fair treat though, sometimes."

"Aha?" The professor was all curiosity at once. "Songs the Sirens sang, eh? It has long been disputed whether these would have been in the Greek diatonic scale or the whole-tone; this might be a discovery of great historical importance. Make her sing, young man."

"She'll need to come out of the bottle for that. Maybe I could put her in your bath?"

"In our swimming-bath," suggested Miss Laura. "The one Edwin is so kindly digging for us. We miss our swims across the Bosphorus," she explained to the professor, "and since our nephew has been pre-scribed digging as a relaxation, he undertook to dig us a pool."

She unbolted the French windows, and the party moved out into the moonlit garden beside the harbour. A frantic figure was shovelling soil at one end of a large pool.

"He's a fashion expert, poor boy," said Miss Ruddock kindly. "Very exacting work."

Edwin straightened from his digging and gazed despairingly at his aunts.

He was at the end of his resources. As a fashion designer, he had reached the peak of the profession; he had invented the Haggard look, and filled London and Paris with haggard beauties; he had invented the K-line and the Swan Bend; he could mould womanhood to his fancy. But now he had run out of ideas. He loved his aunts, but they did not inspire him. Could one inaugurate the Mastodon look, the Monolith look? Hopelessly he returned to his digging.

7

"Have you got the cork out? Now tip her in here," the Professor said. "I'll give her a bar or two on my recorder to start her off."

But Emma needed no starting. As soon as she was tipped into the swimming-pool she began to sing in a tinny croon:

"You may not be an an-gel,
An-gels are all too fe-ew;
But until the day that one comes along
I'll string along with ye-ew . . . "

"Tut-tut," said the professor crossly. "*That's* no use to me, young man." And he turned and went indoors, back to the Madeira, followed by the two Miss Ruddocks.

George stared sadly at Emma in the pool, faced with the prospect of getting her back into the bottle. And what then?

But at this moment Edwin Ruddock came bounding along the bank, filled with new vitality and enthusiasm.

"Is she yours?" he cried. "She's magnificent! I'll give you anything you want for her. The Mermaid look! It'll hit London like a bomb. Let's get her back into the bottle and I'll take her straight up to Bond Street tonight. Makeup, hairstyles—it's all come to me in a flash. What's her name? Emma? Here, Emma, Emma—good girl, come to uncle."

It was George who caught her, Edwin who held the bottle. But Emma, intoxicated by her taste of freedom, did not intend to be corked up again. With a defiant flip of her tail she leapt out of George's arms clean over the harbour wall and disappeared in a silvery splash between a yacht and a trawler.

"Well . . . ," said George; he stifled a huge yawn. "That's that, I reckon. She'll be off home. And I've had all my trouble for nothing."

"Green eyes, silver hair," muttered Edwin distractedly. "Let me get that noted down before I forget it." He rushed indoors for paper and pencil.

George went round to the front of the house and collected his pram. As he pushed it wearily up the hill, it occurred to him for the first time to wonder why a pram had been standing in his porch. Last time he was home it had not been there. But he was too tired to think much about it.

He found the door unlatched and went softly up the dark stairs. Janet stretched a warm, sleepy arm to welcome him, and Sam the cat purred a rampant greeting from the bed-end.

"Ssh . . . ," Janet murmured as he threw his boots at a patch of moonshine. "Remind me to tell you something in the morning. And by the way"—her voice was almost drowned by the purring and the wind outside—"I think it's time we got married."

Reading in Bed

Francis Nastrowski was a young Polish officer. He had once been rich, but was so no longer. Some of the habits of his bygone grandeur still clung to him, however. He was apt to say "Put on my boots" or "Fetch my horse" to whoever was there, even the major, and he was incurably vain, and fond of good wine and reading in bed. Harmless pursuits, one might say, but they nearly led to his downfall.

He was stationed in what had once been the only hotel of a small fishing village. One night when the days drew in, and summer waned, and the tops of the waves began to whiten, he and his friends had a present of burgundy, and on that, together with other, more potent spirits, they managed to become, if not drunk, at least very, very friendly.

Francis at last walked carefully up to bed. His bed was on a balcony, and he found it necessary to snatch up the short stories he was reading and huddle hastily into his chilly sheets. But then he had to get out again in search of a hot-water bottle, and it was several more minutes before he was really comfortable, hugging its warmth, and with a large fold of blanket tucked along his back to prevent draughts.

He had read until one elbow was stiff, and was thinking of turning over onto the other when he heard a noise out beyond the balcony. He raised himself up and looked, for he was becoming momently less sleepy under the influence of cold, fresh air. The hotel faced directly on to the harbour, which was double, with a pier running out in the middle and a lighthouse on the pier.

Francis stared out across the water and finally flashed his torch, which sent a long blue-green ray throbbing down clear to the very bottom. He moved it this way and that, over moored boats and upwards, until it came to rest on the pier, and there, caught in the beam, he saw the Devil sitting very comfortably. He knew it was the Devil because of the impeccable cut of his evening suit, and his horns.

"Well, Francis," called the Devil, "coming across?"

"Just one moment, Devil," replied Francis, who was tucking in his bedclothes to await his return, and he pulled on his breeches and tunic and dived into the dark, glimmering water.

Its coldness was like a blow. It burnt and bruised him, he felt instinctively that he must keep moving as much and as quickly as possible or he would die. So he swam across with wild, hasty strokes until his numbed hands touched the slippery stones of the pier.

The Devil put his cigarette in his mouth, leant over, and gave him a hand up. The hand smelt slightly of brimstone, but he was in no mood to be particular. He straightened himself up, gasping at the warmth of the air. The Devil silently produced a black fur cloak from somewhere and put it on his shoulders. It fitted like a glove and clung round him warmly, giving him an exquisite sensation in his spine.

They sat side by side in silence for some minutes, until the waves and the nodding of boats, which Francis had caused, were gone and the water was quiet once more.

"Would you care to meet my niece?" asked the Devil.

"Any relation of yours, I should be charmed," replied Francis, bowing, and they got up and strolled to the other side of the pier, the Devil carrying his tail negligently over his arm. A boat was waiting there. They stepped into it, and Francis took the oars, which began to move rapidly by themselves.

"Devil, let me congratulate you on a very ingenious idea," said Francis.

The Devil nodded, and they moved forward up the harbour until they came to a flight of steps. Here the boat stopped, spun round twice, and waited while they stepped ashore. It was a part of the town which Francis did not know. They walked along dark cobbled streets, lit here and there by swinging lanterns. There were few lights in the windows. Francis looked in one as he passed; inside an old man was slowly and deliberately swallowing poker after poker. Francis said nothing of this to his companion.

Finally they stopped outside a shop, where a light shone brightly from unshuttered windows. They looked in. It was one of those shops which are found in all old towns and seaside resorts, full of quaint pottery, raffia mats, and wooden calendars with pokerwork dogs on them. Inside, a charming young girl was dancing by herself. She was dressed in an orange overall embroidered with hollyhocks. Her long black plait flew out behind her this way and that as she skipped about the room.

"My niece," said the Devil.

They stepped inside. The girl stopped dancing and came towards them.

"Niece," said the Devil, "This is Lieutenant Francis Nastrowski, a great friend of mine, be polite to him." To Francis he said: "This is my niece, Ola."

"Delighted to meet you," said Francis, bowing. Ola's plait came over her shoulder and patted him on the cheek.

"Will you dance?" she enquired. Before Francis could reply, her plait twined round his neck, and they were spinning giddily round the shop, between the little tables. The Devil sat applauding. Soon they were up through the roof and over the sea. A hundred gulls came circling and shrieking round them, until the whole air seemed white.

"I am giddy. I am going to fall," shouted Francis in the ear of his partner, and he stared down in terror at the sea heaving beneath them. They swooped down towards it, until he could smell the salt of the waves and see fish swimming under the surface with open mouths and goggling eyes.

In the whisk of an eyelid they were back in the shop. Francis sank into a chair with his knees trembling.

"Francis, you're a very fine fellow," said the Devil. "I have admired you for a long time." Francis felt that he ought to rise and bow, but he was too exhausted, and so he merely nodded. "What would you say to becoming my partner and the owner of this charming little shop?" the Devil asked.

Ola smiled and sidled up to the Devil, who patted her head. She began to purr.

"You would receive half the profits and marry my exquisite niece," the Devil went on most persuasively.

"I should be delighted," exclaimed Francis. Suddenly all his exhaustion left him. He rose and danced a mazurka about the room. His black cloak whirled round him, and it seemed that he had an enormous pair of red military boots on, for whenever he clicked his heels and pirouetted, the spurs clashed. Finally he came to rest, balancing accurately on a twisted pewter candlestick.

"Splendid," said the Devil. "We will drink to your future career." He fetched down a dusty bottle and three pink ornamental glasses from cupboard. On each of the glasses was inscribed "A Present from Hell." Francis eyed the bottle with caution. He did not much like the look of the Devil's tipple, which was black, and wondered if he would have a bottle of anything more palatable remaining in one of his pockets. He felt in one and then another. Aha! There was something long and round. But when he pulled it out he found that it was a large garlic sausage.

It then occurred to him that he might deaden the flavour of the Devil's black wine by taking a bite of sausage beforehand, and while the Devil was pouring wine into the glasses he cut off three slices with his silver clasp-knife.

"Can I offer you a slice of garlic sausage?" he asked, offering one politely on the point of the knife.

He did not know that garlic is a very ancient and unfailing specific against wicked spirits. The Devil frowned until his eyebrows came down and met over his nose. Little Ola hissed angrily and came creeping towards him. It was evident that he had offended them. Her black pigtail curled round his throat, but with the end of his strength he threw bits of sausage at them both.

Next morning Lieutenant Nastrowski was found floating in shallow water against the rocks in the lower end of the harbour, with a black cat grasped between his two hands and a strand of seaweed round his neck.

It took him several days to recover from his experience, but the cat never recovered.

Model Wife

It was her pearls that caused the first fight between Dan Thomas and Shani Hughes. They were bound to quarrel anyway, for love and hate boiled between them like treacle and brimstone, but the pearls were at the bottom of it all.

As soon as Dan set eyes on Shani he swore he'd marry her. Dan was a house-painter by trade, and he lived in a cottage up the mountain, the small white one all by itself, with his ladder and his cherry trees and four mountainy cows. Far afield he often travelled, painting men's houses and their barns and or doing a bit of sign-writing, as far afield as Grass Street or Hickson's Hill, for he had a motor scooter that carried him and his gear up the hill roads and through the black belts of forest.

He could do the bold sweep or the detail, paint you roses and curlicues, or finish the west wall of a barn in a day and a half. He bought his groceries wherever he chanced to put on his brakes, so his home village saw him rarely, and Shani, who worked in her Da's dairy, never at all, until the day when the dairy shutters fell down once too often and old Idris Hughes, meeting Dan in the street, ordered a new pair, tongued and grooved and painted with all the beauties that Dan could devise.

A beautiful job he made of them, too, and a galaxy of winsome Jerseys, the goodness shining in their eyes like glycerine, a wreath of roses round each pedigree neck, and silver buckets beside them foaming like an espresso-man's dream. But Dan felt something was lacking and he stamped off down to the village for a conference with old Hughes.

"We need a milkmaid," he shouted before he was halfway inside the door, and then he stopped, for Shani was there, pretty as a bunch of grapes in her green and white stripes, innocent and wild.

She and Dan stared at one another like a couple of cats, and straightway Dan said, "You're the one I want."

"Want for what, pray?" And she went on patting the butter into swans with her butterpats. But the look she gave him was about as simple as the battlefield of Waterloo.

"Want you to sit for me as a model," Dan said, passing a hand over his forehead.

"I'll have to ask my da about that."

In came old Idris just then, and she said to him, "Da, Mr Thomas wants to paint me."

"Modelling fees," grunted Idris Hughes, and Dan nodded. He knew a bargain when he saw one.

Shani preened herself a bit and said, "When shall I come?"

"This evening."

So every evening after work Dan came down and painted her in the dairy, and the milkmaid portrait was the first of many. Shani was small, and she was handsome, but fierce as a wasp, for her mother had died when she was a baby and her da was too busy making money in his dairy to attend to her. She didn't know what it was to be crossed, and he had never put her over his knee and spanked her in his life. Most of the young men in the village thought Dan had bitten off a worse mouthful than Puss when she swallowed the grasshopper.

"What's that?" said Dan, the first evening, painting away. She was fidgeting with something at her neck.

"My pearls," said Shani.

"Tuck them out of sight."

"But they're real pearls," she said, shocked. "My Da's given me one every year of my life, and they're as large as nasturtium seeds."

"I don't care if they're as big as butter-beans. Dairymaids don't wear pearls."

Shani saw the force of this, and she tucked them out of sight under her dress, but the minute painting was done for the evening, out they came again, and she told him, "It's good for pearls to wear them, I read so in the paper. It keeps them lustrous and shining. I've never taken them off since I was born."

"Do you wear them in the bath?" asked Dan, with curiosity.

"In the bath, yes."

"And in bed?" he asked, screwing up his tubes.

"In bed, of course."

"Well! I can tell you one night you won't wear them."

"And what night's that?"

"The night we're wedded," snapped Dan. "I don't fancy going to bed with a string of pearls. Damn it, I wouldn't get a wink of sleep, worrying in case the thing got broken. Pearls in bed would be worse than cake crumbs."

"You'll have to get used to them just the same," flashed back Shani. "I've never taken them off yet, and I'm not going to for you."

Then they took breath and eyed one another, and Dan put his brushes carefully into the turpentine and came over to the counter and gave Shani a kiss that lasted for seven and a half minutes, nonstop, and so concentrated that if they'd been inside a pressure-cooker the gauge would have been hopping up and down in the thousands.

Then he stopped and shook her and said, "You'll take them off."

"I will not!" retorted Shani, but she added, "When shall we get married?"

"In April, when my cherry trees are in flower." For he was a tidy-minded man, and he reasoned that three months would be time enough to get the notion out of her head.

He was wrong, though. From February to April, while the lambs tittupped round their mothers on the slopes and the crocuses began to prink and peer in Dan's garden, dispute flowed between them like a stream in spate. Shani clamoured that she'd wear her virginity the whole of her life sooner than take off those pearls, while Dan shouted that he'd jump off the side of the mountain before he'd wed a girl who thought more of a string of beads than she did of her lover.

The wedding date drew near, and neither had given way an inch. Both secretly hoped that some middle way could be found, for the plain truth was that, rage how they might, could not keep apart; but Dan became black and thunderous, Shani as frosty and brilliant with pride as a raised sword. When they were not kissing, fierce words flew between them like showers of darts.

April came, windy and sunny, and the wedding was celebrated with splendour, for old Idris Hughes was the richest man in the village, and Dan had put by a tidy pile, too, with his painting. The wedding breakfast was to be held in Dan's cottage for the guests to view the glory of his cherry trees, first out on the mountain. As they climbed the steep track the house hung above them, white in a cloud of white, like an egg in a nest of feathers.

"You'll take the pearls off for me tonight, won't you, Shani fach?" said Dan as they strolled up over the grass and he put his arm round her white silk shoulders.

"Indeed and I will not," she snorted. "You can have me in my pearls or you won't have me at all. If you don't like it you can bed yourself in the linhay."

Dan unwound his arm and went on ahead, with jutting brows and a mouth like a ruler, to see to the kettle. The guests crowded after him, gay and curious, into his cottage where many of them had never been before.

All was sanded, spruce, and clean, pots shining like silver, and curtains snowy and smooth. A grand breakfast was laid out on the table, but the guests had eyes for one thing only, and that was a portrait of a fine redheaded wench with eyes like plums and not a stitch of clothes on. The paint was wet, the picture only half finished, and it was plain that Dan must have been painting away at it not half an hour before the wedding. Murmurs and shocked whispers rose up from the party.

"What a hussy! Who is she? Never seen her in the village. Posing in the altogether for him she must have been, not two hours ago. Some stranger from the town she must be. Shameless it is, on his wedding morning."

"Kettle's boiled," said Dan, coming in, brisk and friendly, from the kitchen. "I'll just clear these things into the attic." And he stuck the brushes in a jam-jar, picked up easel and palette, and disappeared for a moment. When he came back he carried a tray with tea, whisky, and brandy.

"Set to, neighbours," he said, and they, remembering the noble meal spread, thought no more of the picture but ate, drank, and joked, while Dan moved among them seeing that each had his need and paying no attention to his bride, who stood bristling in her finery, nearly choked with indignation.

At length the last guest was fed and sped. Dan waved them all off down the steep track.

"Come now," he said. "Walk a bit under the cherry trees, is it, before dark falls?" They were gleaming in the dusk like paper mountains.

"Not a step do I stir," said Shani between her teeth, "till you tell me where you have hidden that good-for-nothing redheaded slut so that I can tear the eyes out of her. Posing on your wedding morning, indeed, with not an inch of cloth to cover her shame! Is it a fool you take me for, Dan Thomas?"

"Indeed, it was only an old page of an illustrated paper I copied her from," Dan said, careless, but there was a guilty note in his voice.

"Tell that to the crows! As if the neighbours would believe such a story. And if you copied it, where have you put the paper?"

"Oh," said Dan, "I tore it up to light the fire for the kettle." And he hummed a bit of tune.

Shani hunted high and low through the length and breadth of the cottage and the orchard and meadow, but not a trace of the intruder could she find. Presently she began to tire. It was a strange way, after all, to spend her wedding evening.

"Tell me it was all a joke now, Danny bach?" she coaxed, coming back to him where he sat in the kitchen, toes to the blaze.

"If I tell you, will you do something for me?" he said, pulling her onto his knee.

"What would that be?" She let her head drop on his shoulder.

"Take those oysters' gallstones off."

She shot up like an electric eel. "And have you give them to the redheaded piece, I suppose," she threw at him. "I'll keep these pearls on till my dying day."

"As long as you do, you can have a bed to yourself," growled Dan, and he gathered up an armful of blankets and made himself a snug bed in the linhay, while Shani fumed herself to sleep in the best room with its patchwork quilt that Dan's granny had made him.

In the morning when she came down, Dan had the breakfast ready and served her as if she had been the Queen herself, but she noticed that the picture of the redheaded girl had been brought down and hung up on the wall.

And moreover, another of the legs had been painted in, and three fingers of the right hand.

Shani said not a word, but she resolved to find the model if it took her a year of searching. Polite as pie she was to Dan, and he to her.

Days went by, and the cherry blossom began to tarnish and scatter. Shani soon found that there was not enough to occupy her in the cottage, for it was a small one, and Dan was out all of most days. So she took to helping her da in the dairy again. Sometimes, when she came home, she would notice that Dan had been back early, and had painted a bit more of the redhead, perhaps a piece of her thigh, or half an arm, or he had touched up the highlight on her knee.

But though fury boiled in Shani, pride kept her lips sealed. Only her eyes snapped and sparkled as they darted over the cottage to see if she could find any trace of her rival, a handkerchief or a hairpin, or even a breath of scent. Never a clue did she find, though, and she began to wonder if the red-haired girl walked naked over the mountain to Dan, making the very sheep blush as they nibbled. Wild dreams haunted her, of shameless, mocking Venuses, and she tossed and turned under the patchwork quilt, while Dan, still sleeping in the linhay, fed load after load of hay to his cows and watched the level get lower and lower. Hard sleeping it would be, soon.

Matters were in this state when the circus from Grass Street came toiling up the slopes of the mountain, to camp in the meadow beyond Shani's da's dairy.

Splendid it was, with a great tent like a piece of white cloud, scarlet-capped elephants, horses with plumes, and all the caravans of the circus folk scattered up and down the meadow painted and decorated as gay as butterflies.

The first that Shani knew of it was the strong man coming into the dairy to ask for his day's ration of three gallons of milk. He gazed at Shani admiringly as she dipped out the milk with her brass dipper. Thin she had grown from searching and pondering, but her cheeks were as pink and her eyes as bright as they had ever been.

"Grand you'd do to be fired from the cannon in the circus tonight," said the strong man. "Our Miss Lightning has the lumbago. Why, you're so light and pretty you'd fly through the air like a thistleblow."

"My husband would never let me," said Shani, but then she thought: Why shouldn't I, just the same? What do I care for him? So she told the strong man she'd come round to the ringmaster's caravan to talk about it.

Mr Blossom was in his shirtsleeves smoking, and he too looked at Shani with admiration. He asked her in for a cup of tea and showed her how to sit with her arms linked round her knees while she was fired from the cannon.

But while he spoke Shani hardly listened, for on his wall was a picture of a woman, decently dressed, but still and for all that the identical redheaded baggage that Dan had painted.

"Who's that?" Shani asked when she could get a word in.

"That?" said Blossom sadly. "That's my poor dear wife, Mrs Blossom."

"Where is she?" demanded Shani, with her fingers tearing feathers out of the cushion.

"She ran away with the tiger-tamer," Mr Blossom sighed.

"And now she's running after my husband. With no clothes on!"

"She couldn't be doing that," Mr Blossom said. "She's been dead these twenty years. One of the tigers got her, poor Blodwen."

"Then how could my husband have painted her picture? With no clothes on?"

"Copied it from somewhere, he must have indeed. Many a picture and likeness used to be taken of my Blodwen. Very beautiful, an artists' model, she was, see? Here's one of her on a toffee tin, and one on a calendar in a crinoline, and here she is before she had her hair cut short."

"And you let her pose like *that?*" Shani said, shocked to the mortal soul.

"Before we were married, that one was. Afterwards she always wore the crinoline."

Shani began to feel bad. She had wronged Dan, suspecting him of carrying on with a woman twenty years in the tiger's stomach. But then she thought: He did it to torment me. And she hardened against him and went with Mr Blossom to learn how to be fired from the cannon, for she was sure that would enrage Dan.

Home at dinnertime she saw that Dan had painted a wreath of daisies round the redhead's neck.

"Take me to the circus tonight, Danny, is it?" she said at dinner, friendly as butter.

"All right," Dan said. "Eat up, girl. Thin as a rake you're growing."

Shani couldn't wait to tell him her news. "Fired from a cannon I'm going to be," she said. "With the mayor and all the neighbours watching. A great honour it is."

"I forbid it!" Dan shouted, banging on the table.

"If I promise not to, will you tell me the gospel truth about that picture?" Shani asked, looking at him with bright eyes.

"If I tell you the truth about the picture, will you take off your pearls for me?"

"Never before I'm in my coffin," stormed Shani.

They parted on evil terms, and Shani went to the circus by herself, but nevertheless Dan was there, too, sitting on a front bench, and Shani saw him and smiled with malice. Dressed all in black she was, in a boiler-suit with a zip from top to toe like a city girl, and round her neck she wore the pearls, shining away like a row of false teeth.

Be damned to her, thought Dan, and he thrust his hands in his pockets and stared moodily at the sawdust.

Outside, night had fallen over the mountain, and the June darkness was as fragrant and spicy as a kitchenful of cloves; red-hot coals of stars blazed overhead.

Drums thundered and trumpets brayed as Shani sat with her hands clasped round her knees and they dropped her into the black mouth of the cannon.

"Stop!" shouted Dan at the last moment. "I can't stand it!" and he rushed forward, but it was too late.

Mr Blossom had pulled the trigger as Dan arrived, and between them they tipped the barrel upwards and Shani was fired straight at the tent roof.

Up, up she soared, and the ancient thin canvas parted with a rending crack as she passed through. She vanished, and the stars received her.

"Quick outside to catch her," cried Blossom, and they poured out into the meadow, but though they searched every inch of ground and found a scattering of pearls, there was never a sign of Shani. "Gone up to heaven she has, direct," they told Dan. "Ah, lucky you were, Thomas, to have a wife that saintly. Honour's been done you, indeed to goodness."

"Compensation I'll have for this," wept Dan, tearing his hair. "She was dearer to me than my right arm, and in another couple of months I'd have tamed her."

"Never mind," they said, comforting him, "better so," and they all went to Blossom's caravan for a drink to drown the solemn thought of Shani, body and all, being lifted up to paradise.

After a while Dan stopped talking about compensation, as he thought of all the trouble he'd had with Shani, and his prickly nights in the linhay. "Women are all the same," said Mr Blossom. "They come and they go. Eaten by tigers or fired out of guns, they're always up to some mischief. It's a man's work that counts. That job you did painting my caravan now, that was a proper bit of work, beautiful. And no pay asked for it either, only an old picture of my Blodwen out of the *Gentleman's Weekly*. Ah, you'll go far, you will, young man."

"Yes, I'll go far," said Dan sadly, and he wandered out of the caravan, for it was late, and started off homewards under the huge stars. But because it was late and he was tired and heartbroken, and could now sleep, if he liked, for ever under the patchwork quilt, he decided not to go home at all, but to spend the night on Shani's da's haystack. Up he climbed, on the feathery warmth of the new hay, and when he reached the top it seemed to him that he was not the only person on that haystack.

"Who's that?" whispered a voice, and he felt a groping hand in the dark. He caught hold of it, tight.

"Shani, is that you?" he asked, and astonishment tipped over the anger in his voice. "What are you doing up here on the stack, giving us all the fright of a lifetime?"

"It's my boiler-suit," said she, between a gulp and a sob. "Came unzippered it did, when I went through the canvas, and fell off onto the tent roof. And I've lost my pearls, too. The old string broke on me and some of them fell into the hay. I've looked and looked and I can find only five. Waiting I was till all the people had gone home before I dared show myself."

"Broke, did it?" said Dan tenderly, turning her round and feeling her to make sure it was true. "Ah there, never mind the old bit of a necklace. Shani, darling, is it? Don't cry then, my pet, my beautiful."

Finding her other hand clenched on the five pearls, he gently opened it and flung them over his shoulder. "Let your da's cows eat them if they've a mind," he said. "We've better things to do than worry after a handful of beads." But because she still wept he promised to buy her another necklace.

Deep in its warmth the haystack held them, and if there were pearls in their bed they never noticed. Nightingales were singing and the stars flared like beacons overhead.

Tomorrow would be midsummer day.

Second Thoughts

☆☆
☆

Miss Dawson was generally wild and haggard-looking, but that Friday morning there was something so strange about her that Miss Pellet at once guessed the worst must have happened. She crossed the road and went up to her.

"Your brother?" she said anxiously, when she was within earshot. "How is he this morning?"

Matilda Dawson turned distraught eyes on her. The worst had happened. The reverend Paul had died in the night.

"How terrible," said Miss Pellett, unaffectedly wiping her eyes, for she had been a great admirer of his, "how terrible for you, my poor Matilda. And what a loss to the village. He was such a friend, such a help to everyone."

Matilda looked at her and said in her deep abrupt voice, "*He* didn't think so."

"What *do* you mean?" Miss Pellett enquired, rather startled. "Everyone has always said that we shall never have a better vicar."

"It was just before he died," Matilda said, wringing her hands dangerously. "I asked him if there was anything he wanted, and he said 'Matilda, I'm not satisfied with myself. If I had my life to live again, I'd live it differently.' 'Nonsense, Paul,' I said, 'you couldn't possibly have been a better vicar in the village. You thought of everyone, you were always working, you never did a thing for yourself. The whole village knows that.' 'No,' he said, 'I might have lived a very different life. I might have done many more things. I'm not content with myself.' And then he sighed again and turned over and died."

She stopped speaking and pulled out her handkerchief.

"But he was a saint," little Miss Pellett cried indignantly, "a regular saint. It's terrible to think of his being dissatisfied with himself. But then, I suppose the truly good always are."

Mrs Maddison took the news of the reverend Paul's last words differently. "Hmm," she said, "he did all he ought, and he knew it. If you ask me, it was just pride made him say that, or else he thought it was the right thing to do. A lot of vicars do say it on their deathbeds, I believe." And she took a cake out of the oven, as though, in her opinion, vicars were a poor lot of hypocrites.

Miss Pellett, though, was much shocked by this attitude, and hurried away to find a more sympathetic listener.

The village mourned him a long time. For it was true that he had been an excellent vicar—hardworking, friendly to everyone, and a figure that they could all look up to. They even pointed him out to strangers, for he was an impressive figure, tall, with white hair, and the face of an ascetic. There was no doubt, no doubt at all, that he was a saint.

"And the little he *eat*," his maid told her mother. "Not enough to keep a bird alive, if you'll credit me."

The new vicar, too, was compared very unfavourably with him. Even Mrs Maddison became more kindly towards his memory.

"At least he looked like a vicar," she said bluntly. "This new one looks more like a plumber if you ask me."

Miss Pellett was most distressed by the change. "Going to church isn't the pleasure it used to be," she said, sighing, and Mrs Henderson and the Misses Guestwick agreed with her.

However, village life must go on, and one must cooperate with the vicar however disagreeable it is. After all, one can always drop in on Miss Pellett, or Miss Lemarchant for a moment or two, to lament over old times. So village life went on, as peacefully as village life ever does, and after a while, what with making the blackberry jam, and the rumour that the Saunderson baby had measles, the reverend Paul Dawson faded into the background. Occasionally Miss Pellett would revive him for a few sad and pleasurable minutes.

"When I think of how I used to see him coming down the village street every day," she would say mournfully. "He always stopped opposite my house, you know, to look over the Coopers' garden wall at that beautiful view. It was always the same. And then he would give himself a little shake, as though to remind himself that there were other things to be done, and go on his way."

And she, too, would shake her head.

But these little plunges into recollection grew fewer and fewer, and by the time the walnuts had all been hulled and put away, and the leaves swept off the lawn, and Christmas was coming, she had resigned herself to her loss in silence.

One day, however, she was leaning from her front window, thinking with a vague melancholy how long it was since she had seen the reverend Paul sharing her beautiful view, when she saw a large black cat walking with an aloof and meditative air along the garden wall on the other side of the road. When it was opposite her window, it sat down with its back to her and looked down across the valley for five or six minutes. Then it rose, gave itself a little shake, and went purposefully on its way. Miss Pellett sighed, and turned again to inspecting the jam and making sure that none was mouldy.

Next day the cat passed again, and the day after. It was not until the day after that that the truth began to dawn in Miss Pellet's mind. Then she went out the door, calling "Pussy, pussy!" but the cat had disappeared.

The day after, she had ready a sardine on a saucer, and she inveigled it into the front hall, and spoke to it passionately, imploring it to vouchsafe an answer.

"Mr Dawson!" And then more boldly, "Paul, Paul, won't you please speak to me?"

But the cat gave her one long, unblinking stare and then walked out of the front door, leaped onto the wall and continued on its way. Every day for a week she gave it a sardine and besought it to speak, but it took no notice, and when the sardine was eaten, would walk out of the door again. But on the eighth day, worn out, probably, by her importuning, it turned, gave her another look, and said coldly, "Well?"

Miss Pellett gasped with joy. The voice was the voice of the reverend Paul. "I knew you!" she exclaimed. "I knew it was you!"

"That wasn't so very difficult, was it?" said Paul. "Anyone might have guessed it, if they'd taken the trouble to look." He fixed her with the eyes of the reverend Paul Dawson, grown green and catlike. "Well, since you've forced me into speaking, what do you want me to say?"

"Oh, but it's so wonderful," cried Miss Pellett ecstatically, "to think you cared for us so much that you have come back to watch over us in your present form."

"I couldn't help where I was born, could I?" said Paul. "It was none of my affair."

Miss Pellett went slightly pink and said, "But it's so comforting, to think that you are still with us, watching over us, the same as you always were."

Paul said nothing to that. He sniffled round the sardine saucer to make sure that nothing was left, and then turned and began to walk towards the door, as though no such creature as Miss Pellett existed in the world.

"Oh," she exclaimed, "but you aren't going, are you?"

"Going?" he said, turning his head and looking past her. "Why not?"

"Well, but," she faltered, "I hoped you'd come and live with me. We have tins of sardines, you know, and it's so cold out."

"I'm afraid that's quite out of the question," Paul said calmly. "I've promised to go and live with Mr Monks and keep down the rats in his workshop. As a personal favour."

Miss Pellet stared at him in horror. Mr Monks was the village carpenter and a shocking character. Mrs Henderson knew the most terrible stories about him, and the idea of the reverend Paul Dawson going to live with him as a personal favour appalled her. Perhaps, though, he intended to convert Mr Monks.

"Does he know who you are?" she asked timidly.

"Good gracious no," Paul said contemptuously. "Do you think I'd tell him a thing like that? It might put him against me. Besides, I have other things to think of than running round telling my life history to every fool."

"But—must you eat rats?" Miss Pellett said rather faintly.

"I enjoy it," Paul answered coldly. He yawned and then ran lightly down the front steps and onto the wall before she could stop him.

Miss Pellett stood looking after him, very much troubled in mind. It was evident that the reverend Paul's saintliness had been somewhat blunted by the cathood which had been superimposed upon it.

But a resolve lit her face. It was clearly her duty to remind him of the true path. It could not take long.

While her courage was still strong, she went alone to call on Mr Monks. She found him in his workshop, and after first looking round to make sure that Paul was nowhere to be seen, she went straight to the point. "That's a fine looking cat you've got, Mr Monks."

"Who, Blackie?" said Mr Monks. "He is that. He's a terror, that cat is, kill anything that walks on two legs he would, give him a chance. Rats, mice, rabbits, birds, pheasants, dogs—all same to him. And fight! There isn't a cat in the village that could stand up to him, not after he's had his saucer of beer in the morning."

"Beer!" said Miss Pellet. "Does he drink beer?"

"I should just about think he does," Mr Monks said. "Puts away as much beer as a Christian, that cat would, and more, too. Wonderful lively he is when he's finished what I give him. And the other day when it was flat, the way he swore! It was a lesson to hear him. Laugh! Me and Mr Sheppard thought we was going to die."

"Is he for sale?" Miss Pellett asked, appalled but nobly sticking to her original plan.

"For sale? Not him," Mr Monks said. "He's valuable to me, that cat is." He winked, and Miss Pellett stumbled out, feeling that life was too much for her. However, she went along to the shop to lay in some more tins of sardines. After all, there was always hope; perhaps the sardines would in the end wean him away from the beer.

In the shop, Miss Lampeter was talking to Mrs Fisher.

"Five chickens gone in a week!" she said furiously. "It's my belief it's that ugly black cat of Mr Monks that takes them. I've seen him sneaking around the run more than once. I'm going to watch for him, and if I catch him, there won't be no questions asked."

Miss Pellett ordered her sardines and went home to bed with a headache.

Paul made no appearance at her house for several says after that, but once she caught sight of him slinking furtively along the wall with a struggling, shrieking bird in his jaws. She thought deeply and passionately for a long time.

Action, however, was taken out of her hands. Next day as she passed by Mr Monks' workshop she heard a furious argument raging inside between Mr Monks and Henry Lampeter. One or two other people seemed to be standing inside also, but which side they were taking she could not discover. She went home and looked over the clean sheets with a distracted mind. It seemed to her that trouble was brewing.

It was when she was shaking a duster out of the window that she saw something that made her blood run cold. Henry Lampeter was walking purposefully down the road with Paul struggling and squalling under his arm, and in his hand was a large stone. Miss Pellett rushed out to intercept him. "You aren't going to kill that cat, surely?" she exclaimed.

"I certainly am," Henry said grimly. "Five of my best layers he took last week, and seven this, besides a couple of young cockerels, just nicely fattening."

"Oh, but you can't," she said in horror. "He's a very valuable cat, and I'm sure if he were kept in for a bit and well fed, he'd stop killing hens. You really mustn't think of such a thing!"

"Sorry, miss," he said. "He's had too many of my chickens for me to feel like letting him off. Besides, once they get the taste of blood, it's hopeless."

Miss Pellett shuddered. He looked so indomitable, holding the scruff of Paul's neck in a firm grip.

At this moment, Mr Monks appeared down the road.

"You've got that cat?" he cried furiously. "You caught that cat without my leave. You'll just hand him over. He's worth money to me. He keeps down the rats better than any terrier."

"Yes, I'll bet he's worth money to you," Henry Lampeter said meaningly, "and my hens are worth money to me. You pay me for my hens, and I'll give you back your cat."

"I'll have the law on you," threatened Mr Monks. "You can't prove it was my Blackie killed your scrubby hens. You ought to build them a better run. If you kill Blackie, you'll have to pay damages!"

"Oh, can't I prove it?" said Henry. "Didn't my old woman see him sneaking round the run with her own eyes? Threw a brick at him, she did, and he hopped it through the hedge as neat as you please!"

"Listen," said Miss Pellett rapidly, "I'll pay you for the hens and take the cat and keep him in so that he can't get out at night. Will you promise me not to kill him? How much were the hens?"

"Well, miss," began Henry, who saw clearly that he would never get any compensation out of Mr Monks, "those hens were valuable birds, and if they get killed, someone ought to pay for them, didn't they?"

"Yes, yes, I'll pay for them," Miss Pellett said, digging feverishly for notes in her bag. She caught a sardonic gleam in Paul's eye as he hung limp under Henry's arm. When she produced the money, he gave a kick and a wriggle and was away over the wall and into some elder bushes before anyone could catch him.

"Well, I'll be damned" said Henry angrily, staring first after Paul, and then at his arm, where the blood was beginning to well in three long scratches. "I warn you, miss, if that cat takes any more of my hens, I won't answer for the consequences." He dropped the stone and moved off down the road.

"And what about me?" Mr Monks demanded indignantly. "Have my Blackie taken away from me without a by-your-leave? He was a fine ratter, that cat was."

She paid him also.

It wasn't easy to find Paul, but she caught him that evening, stalking a starling by the cucumber frames. She took him indoors and fed him enormously, in the hope that it would check his appetite for chicken hunting. Then, rather self-consciously, she produced a little silver bowl of water, held him firmly by the scruff of the neck, and sprinkled some of it over his forehead, saying, "In the name of the Father, the Son, and the Holy Ghost, I baptise you Paul Dawson."

Paul gave himself a shake and looked at her furiously.

"What the devil do you think you're doing?" he said. "You might give me pneumonia." And he washed his face violently, first with one paw, and then with the other.

Miss Pellett sighed. The christening did not seem to have had the beneficial effect that she had hoped.

However, that night, and for two or three nights after, Paul seemed somnolent and willing enough to stay in. She gave him so much to eat that he was becoming plump, but remained very taciturn.

One day as he was sitting gazing into the fire, and she was talk-ing to him, begging him to reform—she had even tried reading him passages from the New Testament, but something in his attitude as he listened made her decide to stop—there was a knock at the door, and Mrs Henderson and Miss Lemarchant walked in.

"Did I hear you talking to someone?" asked Miss Lemarchant.

Miss Pellett threw concealment to the winds and told them the whole story. By the end, Mrs Henderson was beginning to look signif-icantly at Miss Lemarchant, but just then Paul spoke, more to himself than to anybody else. "Women," he said. "There's no pleasing them. Either they won't believe anything, or else they lose their heads and begin looking out for fandangles like angels on the roof."

It was not evident which part of this remark applied to whom, but from the long, sour look that he gave Miss Pellett before returning to his firegazing, it was evident that some of it, at least, was directed against her.

The other two were speechless with amazement, but could hardly help being convinced. "His poor sister! Whatever would she say?" exclaimed Miss Lemarchant. "It's just as well she's gone to live in Putney."

Paul gave a snort of laughter. "So that's where she's gone," he remarked. "Matilda was always a fool."

By the end of the morning, Mrs Madison and the Guestwick sisters had also heard the news, and dropped in separately to verify it. At lunchtime Paul was in a very bad temper.

"I knew how it would be," he said. "They think I'm the savior of the village all over again. They'll be asking me to kiss the babies and be Father Christmas at the schoolchildren's party next. I'm off."

And before Miss Pellett could prevent him, he leapt through the window and was gone.

A shocking chapter of slaughter among the hens followed, and by the end of two weeks at least five men in the village were publicly out for his blood, in spite of Miss Pellet's supplications. No one had seen him, though, except a few children who had flung stones after him in the street, but could not catch him.

On Christmas Eve, Miss Pellett had a small party—just Mrs Henderson, Mrs Maddison, Miss Lemarchant, and the Guestwick sisters. By a tacit agreement no one raised the painful subject of Paul, though once they came perilously near it when Miss Lemarchant remarked "Dear me! Last Christmas this time! That beautiful service! So touching!"

Mrs Henderson looked warningly at her, and Miss Pellett went hastily out of the room to fetch more mince pies.

As she stood in the larder, it seemed to her that she saw two green eyes staring in from outside. She went to the back door and called, "Paul? Paul?"

A black form slid past her and went striding into the drawing room. When she followed with her plate of mince pies she found Paul, with his tail swishing angrily, sitting in the middle of the circle.

"Why didn't you tell me all these people were here?" he said rudely.

"You didn't ask me," she apologized.

"Dear Mr Dawson," exclaimed the younger Miss Guestwick boldly, "now that you are here, won't you say a few Christmas words to us?"

"Christmas words!" He spat out a catlike expression of scorn and, turning his back on them all, sat and stared into the fire.

"Mr Dawson," pleaded Miss Lemarchant, "can't you see the error of your ways? Can't you see what a terrible life you are leading, the more so because of the beauty of what went before? Can't you see how you would enhance that beauty by looking after us again in your present form?" She stopped, amazed at her own eloquence, but the cat gave no sign of having heard.

"Bah! What he needs is a good spanking," said Mrs Maddison. "I'd give him one if he were mine. I always said the man was a hypocrite." She looked at him vengefully.

The others, however went on imploring him to mend his ways, until Paul grew impatient.

"Oh hiss to all you old hens!" he said irritably. "I never did a thing that was worthwhile when I was the vicar, and now, just when life is beginning to be enjoyable, you all start in on me. But you can talk till you're black in the face without making any difference. I've never had such a good time before. I live on the fat of the land, not a tom in the village dares stand up to me, and I have thirteen families of kittens. There's Christmas sentiment for you! Which reminds me, I haven't made arrangements about my turkey yet. I hear there are some good ones at the farm over in Little Linden. Ten past eleven? I must be going."

In the horrified silence that followed, he walked to the door, waited unblinkingly until it was opened for him, and then passed rapidly through.

They never saw him again.

On Christmas morning, as she walked up to the church, Miss Pellett heard old Steggle the sexton talking to Henry Lampeter. "I went into the church good and early to put it to rights, like," he rasped in his creaky old voice, "and what did I see but Mr Monk's Blackie, that good-for-nothing animal. He scuttered away down the aisle fast enough when he saw me. Ar! And what d'you think 'e'd bin doin' 'Enry?" He leaned nearer to Lampeter, and whispered stridently. "'E'd bin sitting on the table where the 'ymn books is kept, tearing them up with 'is claws. Whad'you make of that, eh? If you arsk me," he finished portentously, "that cat is the devil 'imself."

Miss Pellett knew better.

Girl in a Whirl

Her name was Daisy and she was a smasher, the crispest colleen in Killyclancy. Only, as misfortune would have it, old Mr Mulloon said she was unlucky, he having met her once in the street and gone home to find his finest fowl drowning in a puddle; brandy had revived it, true, but anyway those looks weren't natural, Mr Mulloon said. Whoever heard of hair like spun milk atop of a pair of eyes black as sloes? Depend on it, the girl was an albinoess, cunningly covering up a pair of cherry-pink pupils with smoked contact lenses.' And everyone knew albinos had the Evil Eye.

His croaks of warning were much heeded by the mothers of Killyclancy, and three weeks afterwards Daisy found she might as well look for blackberries in April as find a young fellow to take her to so much as a cheeseparing party. After some rebuffs, she began to have a positive hate for the male sex, and never laughed so hearty as when one of the creatures had his car stall on him at the traffic lights, or dropped a bagful of carpet-tacks in the Market Square.

There were two men in the town, though, who took an interest in Daisy. One of them was the doctor. More of him later. The other was Con O'Leary, who ran the Housewives' Help Service in the day-time and sang in opera at night. Housewives loved him for the bits of *Traviata* that would come carolling out from under the sink as he scrubbed, or *Trovatore* from the upper storey.

41

He had a little helicopter from which he used to clean the windows with a long-handled mop, and thus he was in a position to know that old Mr Mulloon's theory as to Daisy's pupils and the possibility of her hair being a wig was wrong: quite wrong. He had seen her in her bath one never-to-be-forgotten Valentine's eve, and since then he was a changed being; staggered sometimes as he walked, like one in a daze, undercharged several housewives for cleaning down their paintwork, and sang A flat instead of A natural in the middle of *Adelaide*. He was in love, in fact.

He never missed Daisy's act. Fortunately the variety turns came on before the townsfolk settled to the serious opera or drama of the evening. Made up as Acis, or Don Pasquale, he could watch enthralled as she came onto the stage in her white silk costume all printed over with huge black marguerites.

The Dome of Death, it was called. Leaping nonchalantly on her motorbike, Daisy would whizz round a couple of times to get warmed up on the lower lip of the great aluminium funnel, and then suddenly—flip!—she'd be horizontal, flying round inside it like a fly in a pudding-bowl and slowly circling upwards, little by little, all the time calm and bored-looking as if she were doing the kids' crossword in an evening paper, quite regardless of the fact that one sputter from her engine would drop her twisting down to annihilation.

After a while she'd reach the top and swing there, looping like a crazy white bangle on the twirl round an invisible wrist. Then she'd begin to slow and drop, circling lower, until at last she ran slanting onto the ground in a wide curve. Girl and bike came vertical once more and the engine kicked to a halt. Daisy would bow once to the applause and walk off, wiping her hands on a clean bit of cotton waste, unsmiling.

She never changed at the theatre but slung a dark coat on and went straight home. And oh, the many times that Con would have wished to see her home, and he with only six or seven minutes to his call.

One Sunday, though, restless and fretful from his landlady's good dinner, he put on his best suit that was purple as a Pershore plum and went knocking at her door.

When she opened, he was tongue-tied and stood like a rock gazing at his bootlaces.

"Well?" she said. She was a grand sight to see, with her hair, just washed, spraying out in all directions like a dandelion-clock, but Con was so tangled up in his intention that he had no eyes for her.

"I wondered if I might," he began, and then he faltered, lost courage, and ended up, "might have left a bucket here last Tuesday week when I washed the distemper?"

"Took you long enough to miss it, faith," said Daisy, ironic. "Well, you didn't."

"Then perhaps," he went on doggedly, "perhaps a bar of yellow soap?"

"Neither yellow soap, nor pink, nor green, nor white," said Daisy. "After I'd paid your ten shillings, I had a fine old clear-round getting rid of the muddy footprints of you."

"Then maybe 'twas my stepladder that I've been seeking the length of the town?" he suggested, but with despair in his voice. She took a step back and began to close the door.

"No, wait," said Con in agony. "Perhaps—perhaps you'd kindly consider marrying me?"

She looked him over from top to toe, her eyes fairly blazing with scorn.

"Shall I tell you what I admire, Con O'Leary?" she said, speaking slow and biting. "What I admire most in the world is courage. Look at you, standing there with your white face and your shaking hand. Begorra, there's not an inch of courage in the whole footage of ye."

And this time she did shut the door, and left Con on the outside of it.

Now she was unfair, had she but known it. Though he never went out of his way to show it, Con was as brave a man as any in the town, only for the little matter of the courting. 'Twas common knowledge the way he'd rescued old Mr Mulloon from the church tower, and him with the drink taken. He was bold as a lion with the housewives, did they try to flirt with him in corners or haggle down his price, and the way he cleaned windows was a wonder to all, jumping over the ten-foot gap from his helicopter to the sill for a final polish, leaving the machine to hover by itself, and then jumping back again with the duster the way you'd be thinking he was a chamois, and no notice taken of twenty foot of emptiness under the soles of his boots. Indeed, he had been given free membership of the Daredevils' Club, though he seldom went to the meetings and thought them great foolishness.

That evening, though, sore and spurned from head to heel, he took a fancy to attend. All the bold young sparks of the town belonged, and he felt the need for company. When he got there they were in a fine distraction and turbulence.

"Look what's come in it, will you!" exclaimed Michael Whelan. "'Tis herself, the unchancy one, has sent in an application to be considered for membership. Yerra, what then, at all?"

"Is it Daisy you mean?"

"Ah, 'tis. And a fine misfortune 'twould be for the lot of us did she set foot in the club. Many's the death she'd encompass, whether in the rock climbing or the dirt-track riding or the swimming or the horse-breaking. And a woman, at that! That I should ever live to see the day! 'Tis not to be considered."

"She must have a trial, though," said Danny Mayhew, president of the club. "The rules have it so. A fair trial to anyone applying, they say."

Con sat silent, for he was unhappy in his mind, while the men discussed in shocked voices what trial would ensure Daisy's failure.

"Look at it this way," said Michael. "Sure, we wish no harm to the girleen, for what's a bit of an Evil Eye when there's goodwill in it?

'Tis how we must be thinking of some grand and terrible exploit will daunt her entirely, the way she'll not even attempt it."

"Ah, sha, he has the marrow of it," said several approving voices.

Danny said, "We could ask her to ride her bike on a tightrope across the Deeps of Kilglore."

"She might agree," Michael pointed out. "'Twould be no unaccustomed thing for her, waltzing over the tightrope the way she do when the Dome of Death's dismantled for the de-rusting."

"But the Deeps of Kilglore, man! She'd never dare. And the river's risen lately, with the deal of rain we've been having. 'Tis a fearsome place."

"Supposing she tried it, and fell?"

"Sure then, wouldn't we have Con here at hand with his grand little broth of a plane to scoop her up like a hurley ball?"

Con was startled, but after a minute he thought, Well, why not? Maybe she'd be grateful then. Maybe she'd run to his arms, crying out, "My hero!" Maybe she'd give up this unwomanish notion. Maybe 'twas not a bad suggestion at all.

The club was unanimous in approval of the plan.

It was a sharp, gray day, the Saturday fixed for the trial. The sky had rained itself out and blown itself dry. Leaves and trees shone with a glitter and heeled over, and a bitter white wind drove a flock of cloud scurrying to the west.

Half the town had assembled near the Deeps of Kilglore, for, since Daisy's scornful acceptance of the club's terms, the news of the test had somehow got abroad. To be sure, the club's activities were strictly against the law, but, as the sergeant said, "A bit of a ducking will do the girleen no harm at all, and maybe souse the Evil Eye out of her. And the more souls there is watching, the more to catch her if she falls."

It was a fearsome place, indeed. The club members had already strung a cable across the Deeps, the high gorge where the Kildeggan river arched its back before plunging over the falls into St. Piumail's pool, reputed bottomless. The heavy rains had swollen the river to a torrent and the roar of it would have overshouted Gabriel's trump.

Daisy was as white as a wand but calm enough, as Danny Mayhew tested the cable and Michael Whelan helped wheel the bike to the cliff's lip. Con kept himself out of sight, hovering round the windward side of a rock point, for he could not bear the torture of watching her start. The cable ran cut across the gorge, slender and silver as a spiderweb, and on this he fixed his eyes.

All at once it trembled, as the web does when the spiderwife's at home, and a moment later the little shining toy ran out and down, more like a raindrop on a telegraph wire than a live creature balancing over death and vacancy.

Con brought his helicopter alongside. He had no fear of startling Daisy, for, though he felt he could hear his own distracted breathing, the roar of the falls drowned even the sound of his engine.

Daisy was halfway across now. Just as she began the slow climb to the opposite cliff her bike seemed to slip and stagger.

A sort of a sigh went through the watching multitude as the machine wavered to the right. She brought it back, and then, slowly as a leaf fluttering down, the front wheel slid to the left and the bike dangled crossways over the cable for a full half second while Daisy catapulted head over heels into space and down in a leisurely curve towards the white teeth of the pool.

Con dropped like a stone after her and had her snapped up in his nylon catch-net before she'd fallen more than thirty feet. It was a noble catch. The cheer that went up from the watchers might have been heard from Dublin to Doon Point.

The sergeant hugged Danny Mayhew, Michael Whelan beat old Mr Mulloon on the back and pulled a black bottle out of his pocket. Only the doctor looked thoughtful as Con pitched his helicopter back to the clifftop.

Con had drawn in his net and now gently let Daisy down to the ground while he hovered; the doctor unloosed her and then Con landed alongside.

"All right is she, man dear?" he called.

He was not prepared for what followed.

"*Oh!* You—you meddling fool!" Daisy stormed at him. "Swooping up like a half-witted hen, you! Puffed with your conceit and insolence! Why couldn't you let me fall? That would have been better than to live the laughing-stock of the town, rescued like a sausage spitted by the kind courtesy of the cook. What'll I do now, answer me that?— I'll never be able to lift up my head again."

And first she broke out crying—then she slapped Con's face, and then fell fainting to the ground.

"She's dead!" Con shrieked at the doctor.

"No, asleep," the doctor contradicted. "Shock's all that's in it with her. I'll take her to my home and give her a sleeping-tablet that'll settle her sounder than a babe in arms."

And far from the roystering crowd he took her, though several voices were heard to murmur that a dram from Michael's black bottle would suit the case better and maybe put some cheer into the colleen.

When she woke up she was on the doctor's couch in the doctor's beautiful house, and the doctor was handing her a cup of tea, the strangest-tasting brew she'd ever laid lip to.

"Ah there, poor dear," the doctor said to his sister. "She'll be better in the blink of an eye."

He was a striking-looking man, Dr. Phillimore Madrassi, tall, lean, and black-haired as the devil, with a gleam in his eye. Behind him stood the old-maid sister, Miss Merlwyn, with a flat, square face like the back end of a tin loaf, and a bit of black hair atop, as if the loaf had been burnt. Daisy had the concern on her, looking at the pair of them.

"How are you?" creaked Miss Merlwyn.

Daisy struggled round and sat up. Rare and lovely the doctor's room was, with Sheraton, Chippendale, and Venetian glass, the walls as delicate as a duck's egg and the Persian carpet all dove and rose. But the first sight that struck Daisy's eye was her own feet in sneakers all covered with dust and oil, planted in the middle of this carpet that was worth a queen's ransom. She tried to hide them out of sight.

"Lie down again now, let you," the doctor said. "You're not well enough to be moving yet."

Daisy wanted to go home, but he said no to this. He wanted to study her reactions, he said.

"Fine goings-on!" exclaimed Agnes, the doctor's maid. "Half a dozen boluses and a pint of linseed oil, Mr O'Shaughnessy, if you please. He sits by her bed, the poor young creature, questioning away like the Judge himself, and she with no more strength to refuse than a day-old chick. All about did her mother shut her in a dark cupboard when she was a gossoon and suchlike."

"Is this seemly, Phillimore?" Miss Merlwyn asked her brother gloomily. "Suppose some of our titled patients should come to the house?"

The doctor gave his wolfish grin. "I'll worry about that when it happens," he said. "Leave me alone now, my dear, will you, to cure the girl's man-hate on her, and study the grandest case of obsessive fixation and traumatic syndrome it's ever been my lot to meet."

"Oh, traumatic fiddlestick!" Miss Merlwyn barked angrily. "That white-headed piece has you clean bewitched." And she flounced back to her petit point.

The doctor sat down again beside Daisy. It may have been his questing his way through the whole of her life, or merely the human talk of a male creature, but devil a doubt she was looking better, the eyes brighter on her and the cheeks pinker than they had been for days.

"I feel sorry for that Con O'Leary," she suddenly remarked. "I'm sorry I slapped his face."

"Ah, never mind him," said the doctor. "I want to try an experiment on you."

"What's that?" asked Daisy as he strapped a metal band studded with knobs into position on her arm.

"I invented it myself," said the doctor, easy and affable, switching on a battery. "It's a little thing to take the measure of your mood. I want to find out are you still in a state of shock."

In his hand he held a dial with a needle that jerked and flickered, and now, keeping his eye on it, he reached and kissed Daisy's cheek. She didn't twitch an eyelid. The needle moved slowly from thirty to forty.

"Still some shock present," said the doctor professionally, making a note. "We'll try again."

This time he kissed her on the lips, and the needle rose up to sixty.

Meanwhile old Mr Mulloon was feeling ill at ease. True, Daisy had put the Evil Eye on his hen. True, O'Leary had been ready to rescue her, so no great harm had been done, but had it been right, he asked himself, to smear axle-grease quite so thickly on that cable? He very much feared not.

Seeking guidance on the matter, old Mr Mulloon returned to the Deeps of Kilglore and sat brooding on the cliff. Maybe some means of atonement would come into his head.

The season's heavy rains, washing and washing down the falls, had ended by turning St. Piumail's pool to a whirlpool that swung and turned like a great cone of black glass beyond the dizzying roar of the waterfall. It was a wonderful thing, a thing of portent.

Gazing at it, Mr Mulloon observed something going round and round, and after a minute he recognized this as Daisy's motorbike.

"All her livelihood, the poor colleen, God save her," he said, shocked.

"Maybe if I climbed onto that rock and leaned out with my crooked stick I could fetch it to land."

"Holy mercy!" exclaimed Daisy. The pointer on the dial leapt and quivered at a hundred and twenty, and she fetched the doctor a clip on the ear. Agnes, listening at the keyhole, decided it was time to intervene.

"Doctor, Doctor!" she cried, bursting in—and wouldn't this make a grand tale for the town—"old Mr Mulloon's fallen himself into the awesome great whirlpool! Half the town's up at the pool of Piumail watching the poor man spinning round out of reach, and he the innocentest creature that ever breathed a word of malice in Killyclancy, bless his evil, drunken old heart."

While she spoke she eyed with interest Daisy's scarlet cheeks and furious eyes. The girl was struggling to free herself from the doctor's contraption.

"You're cured," he said hastily, rubbing his ear. "Stay here quietly till I get back. Another night under sedatives—"

"I'm coming up to the pool," said Daisy, and strode past him to the door.

Up at the pool of St. Piumail the townsfolk were gathered again. There had not been so many free spectacles since King Conor's dairy show and the events leading up to the war of the Dun Cow.

Old Mr Mulloon went round and round, quite self-possessed—someone had thrown him a bottle of the stuff tied onto a piece of cork—but he was getting lower in the whirlpool all the time, and when he reached the bottom, what then?

"He's done for," said the doctor, staring down the long, black glass slope at the little foreshortened figure so far below. "Nothing can reach him down there."

"Yes, it can!" cried Daisy. "Who'll lend me a motorbike? I'll go down for him myself!"

And before anyone could cry "Stop!" she had grabbed Danny Mayhew's Smith-Rivers, kicked it into life, and plunged onto the lip of the whirlpool.

"Daisy!" shouted the doctor angrily. He had not planned to cure her for this.

But already she was swinging round, vertical to the glossy slope of the water, calm and debonair as ever in her act, and all the time going lower and lower in pursuit of Mr Mulloon, who sat below her as if in an armchair, gazing up with a disbelieving expression on his face.

She leaned over, she grabbed him, she dumped him behind her on the pillion.

"Isn't it a wonderful thing," he remarked to himself. "Seized up by the scruff, like she was the young Lochinvar coming out of the west to save him. Eh, it's a wild age we live in."

For the spectators above, though, it was plain that the weight of two riders was going to be too much for the aged Smith-Rivers. Daisy herself realized this and tried to coax more speed from the flagging machine. No use. Her despairing glance flung up, and then fixed. Overhead, calmly unloosing his catch-net as if this were old routine, was Con O'Leary, dropped as far down into the whirlpool's maw as the spread of his rotors would allow.

"Holy Pate," said the people of Killyclancy, "he'll save the pair of them yet. Ah, it's the grand lad he is, entirely. Watch him dangle for them now, 'tis as good as bobbing for apples. Wurra, he's missed. Try on the next round, boyo! Cunningly does it, the way the monkey caught the alligator's tail. Ah, he's got them. Now, will she be dealing Con another of thim great tempestuous slaps? 'Twill be a gradle thing to see."

But in this respect the onlookers were disappointed. Dropped from the helicopter, Daisy did not wait for Con's cautious approach. She disentangled herself from Mr Mulloon, rushed on Con with open arms, enveloped him in a smothering hug, and cried out, "My hero!"

In the background the doctor scowled, defeated. His cure had been successful, but he was not the man to appreciate it.

Hair

Tom Orford stood leaning over the rail and watching the flat hazy shores of the Red Sea slide past. A month ago he had been watching them slide in the other direction. Sarah had been with him then, leaning and looking after the ship's wake, laughing and whispering ridiculous jokes into his ear.

They had been overflowingly happy, playing endless deck games with the other passengers, going to the ship's dances in Sarah's mad, rakish conception of fancy dress, even helping to organise the appalling concerts of amateur talent, out of their gratitude to the world.

"You'll tire yourself out!" somebody said to Sarah as she plunged from deck-tennis to swimming in the ship's pool, from swimming to dancing, from dancing to Ping-Pong. "As if I could," she said to Tom. "I've done so little all my life, I have twenty-one years of accumulated energy to work off."

But just the same, that was what she had done. She had died, vanished, gone out, as completely as a forgotten day, or a drift of the scent of musk. Gone, lost to the world. Matter can neither be created nor destroyed, he thought. Not matter, no. The network of bones and tendons, the dandelion clock of fair hair, the brilliantly blue eyes that had once belonged to Sarah, and had so riotously obeyed her will for a small portion of her life—a forty-second part of it, perhaps—was now quietly returning to earth in a Christian cemetery in Ceylon. But her spirit, the fiery intention which had coordinated that machine of flesh and bone and driven it through her life—the spirit, he knew, existed neither in air nor earth. It had gone out, like a candle.

He did not leave the ship at Port Said. It was there that he had met Sarah. She had been staying with friends, the Acres. Orford had gone on a trip up the Nile with her. Then they had started for China. This was after they had been married, which happened almost immediately. And now he was coming back with an address, and a bundle of hair to give to her mother. For she had once laughingly asked him to go and visit her mother, if she were to die first.

"Not that she'd enjoy your visit," said Sarah drily. "But she'd be highly offended if she didn't get a lock of hair, and she might as well have the lot, now I've cut it off. And you could hardly send it to her in a registered envelope."

He had laughed, because then death seemed a faraway and irrelevant threat, a speck on the distant horizon.

"Why are we talking about it, anyway?" he said.

"Death always leaps to mind when I think of Mother," she answered, her eyes dancing. "Due to her I've lived in an atmosphere of continuous death for twenty-one years."

She had told him her brief story. When she reached twenty-one, and came into an uncle's legacy, she had packed her brush and comb and two books and a toothbrush ("All my other possessions, if they could be called mine, were too ugly to take."), and, pausing only at a hairdressers' to have her bun cut off (he had seen a photograph of her at nineteen, a quiet, dull-looking girl, weighed down by her mass of hair), she had set off for Egypt to visit her only friend, Mrs Acres. She wrote to her mother from Cairo. She had had one letter in return.

"My dear Sarah, as you are now of age I cannot claim to have any further control over you, for you are, I trust, perfectly healthy in mind and body. I have confidence in the upbringing you received, which furnished you with principles to guide you through life's vicissitudes. I know that in the end you will come back to me."

"She seems to have taken your departure quite lightly," Orford said, reading it over her shoulder.

"Oh, she never shows when she's angry," Sarah said. She studied the letter again. "Little does she know," was her final comment, as she put it away. "Hey, I don't want to think about her. Quick, let's go out and see something—a pyramid or a cataract or a sphinx. Do you realise that I've seen absolutely nothing—nothing—nothing all my life? Now I've got to make up for lost time. I want to see Rome and Normandy and Illyria and London—I've never been there, except Heath Row—and Norwegian fjords and the Taj Mahal."

Tomorrow, Orford thought, he would have to put on winter clothes. He remembered how the weather had become hotter and hotter on the voyage out. Winter to summer, summer to winter again.

London, when he reached it, was cold and foggy. He shrank into himself, sitting in the taxi which squeaked and rattled its way from station to station, like a moving tomb. At Charing Cross he ran into an acquaintance who exclaimed, "Why, Tom old man, I didn't expect to see you for another month. Thought you were on your honeymoon or something?"

Orford slid away into the crowd.

"And can you tell me where Marl End is?" he was presently asking at a tiny, ill-lit station which felt as if it were in the middle of the steppes.

"Yes, sir," said the man, after some thought. "You'd best phone for a taxi. It's a fair way. Right through the village and on over the sheepdowns."

An aged Ford, lurching through the early winter dusk, which was partly mist, brought him to a large red-brick house, set baldly in the middle of a field.

"Come back and call for me at seven," he said, resolving to take no chances with the house, and the driver nodded, shifting his gears, and drove away into the fog as Orford knocked at the door.

The first thing that struck him was her expression of relentless, dogged intention. Such, he thought, might be the look on the face of a coral mite, setting out to build up an atoll from the depths of the Pacific.

He could not imagine her ever desisting from any task she had set her hand to.

Her grief seemed to be not for herself but for Sarah.

"Poor girl. Poor girl. She would have wanted to come home again before she died. Tired herself out, you say? It was to be expected. Ah well."

Ah well, her tone said, it isn't my fault. I did what I could. I could have prophesied what would happen; in fact I did; but she was out of my control, it was her fault, not mine.

"Come close to the fire," she said. "You must be cold after that long journey."

Her tone implied he had come that very night from Sarah's cold un-Christian deathbed, battling through frozen seas, over Himalayas, across a dead world.

"No, I'm fine," he said. "I'll stay where I am. This is a very warm room." The stifling, hothouse air pressed on his face, solid as sand. He wiped his forehead.

"My family, unfortunately, are all extremely delicate," she said, eyeing him. "Poor things, they need a warm house. Sarah—my husband—my sister—I daresay Sarah told you about them?"

"I've never seen my father," he remembered Sarah saying. "I don't know what happened to him—whether he's alive or dead. Mother always talks about him as if he were just outside in the garden."

But there had been no mention of an aunt. He shook his head.

"Very delicate," she said. She smoothed back her white hair, which curved over her head like a cap, into its neat bun at the back.

"Deficient in thyroid—thyroxin, do they call it? She needs constant care."

Her smile was like a swift light passing across a darkened room.

"My sister disliked poor Sarah—for some queer reason of her own—so all the care of her fell on me. Forty years."

"Terrible for you," he answered mechanically.

The smile passed over her face again.

"Oh, but it is really quite a happy life for her, you know. She draws, and plays with clay, and of course she is very fond of flowers and bright colours. And nowadays she very seldom loses her temper, though at one time I had a great deal of trouble with her."

I manage all, her eyes said, I am the strong one, I keep the house warm, the floors polished, the garden dug, I have cared for the invalid and reared my child, the weight of the house has rested on these shoulders and in these hands.

He looked at her hands as they lay in her black silk lap, fat and white with dimpled knuckles.

"Would you care to see over the house?" she said.

He would not, but could think of no polite way to decline. The stairs were dark and hot, with a great shaft of light creeping round the corner at the top.

"Is anybody there?" a quavering voice called through a half-closed door. It was gentle, frail, and unspeakably old.

"Go to sleep, Miss Whiteoak, go to sleep," she called back. "You should have swallowed your dose long ago."

"My companion," she said to Orford, "is very ill."

He had not heard of any companion from Sarah.

"This is my husband's study," she told him, following him into a large, hot room.

Papers were stacked in orderly piles on the desk. The bottle of ink was half full. A half-written letter lay on the blotter. But who occupied this room? "Mother always talks as if he were just outside."

On the wall hung several exquisite Japanese prints. Orford exclaimed in pleasure.

"My husband is fond of those prints," she said, following his glance. "I can't see anything in them myself. Why don't they make objects the right size, instead of either too big or too small? I like something I can recognise, I tell him."

Men are childish, her eyes said, and it is the part of women to see that they do nothing foolish, to look after them.

They moved along the corridor.

"This was Sarah's room," she said.

Stifling, stifling, the bed, chair, table, chest all covered in white sheets. Like an airless graveyard waiting for her, he thought.

"I can't get to sleep," Miss Whiteoak called through her door. "Can't I come downstairs?"

"No, no, I shall tell you when you may come down," the old lady called back. "You are not nearly well enough yet!"

Orford heard a sigh.

"Miss Whiteoak is wonderfully devoted," she said as they slowly descended the stairs. "I have nursed her through so many illnesses. She would do anything for me. Only, of course, there isn't anything that she can do now, poor thing."

At the foot of the stairs an old, old woman in a white apron was lifting a decanter from a sideboard.

"That's right, Drewett," she said. "This gentleman will be staying to supper. You had better make some broth. I hope you are able to stay the night?" she said to Orford.

But when he explained that he could not even stay to supper, she took the news calmly.

"Never mind about the broth, then, Drewett. Just bring in the sherry."

The old woman hobbled away, and they returned to the drawing room. He gave her the tissue-paper full of Sarah's hair.

She received the bundle absently, then examined it with a sharp look. "Was this cut before or after she died?"

"Oh—before—before I married her." He wondered what she was thinking. She gave a long, strange sigh, and presently remarked, "That accounts for everything."

Watching the clutch of her fat, tight little hands on the hair, he began to be aware of a very uneasy feeling, as if he had surrendered something that only now, when it was too late, he realised had been of desperate importance to Sarah. He remembered, oddly, a tale from childhood: "Where is my heart, dear wife? Here it is, dear husband: I am keeping it wrapped up in my hair."

But Sarah had said, "She might as well have the lot, now I've cut it off."

He almost put out his hand to take it back; wondered if, without her noticing, he could slip the packet back into his pocket.

Drewett brought in the sherry in the graceful decanter with a long, fine glass spout at one side. He commented on it.

"My husband bought it in Spain," she said . "Twenty years ago. I have always taken great care of it."

The look on her face gave him again that chilly feeling of uneasiness. "Another glass?" she asked him.

"No, I really have to go." He looked at his watch and said with relief, "My taxi will be coming back for me in five minutes."

There came a sudden curious mumbling sound from a dim corner of the room. It made him start so violently that he spilt some of his sherry. He had supposed the place empty, apart from themselves.

"Ah, feeling better, dear?" the old lady said.

She walked slowly over to the corner and held out a hand, saying, "Come and see poor Sarah's husband. Just think—she had a husband—isn't that a queer thing?"

Orford gazed aghast at the stumbling slobbering creature that came reluctantly forward, tugging away from the insistent white hand.

His repulsion was the greater because in its vacant, puffy-eyed stare he could detect a shadowy resemblance to Sarah.

"She's just like a child, of course," said the old lady indulgently. "Quite dependent on me, but wonderfully affectionate, in her way." She gave the cretin a fond glance. "Here, Louisa, here's something pretty for you! Look, dear—lovely hair."

Dumbly, Orford wondered what other helpless, infirm pieces of humanity might be found in this house, all dependent on the silver-haired old lady who brooded over them, sucking them dry like a gentle spider. What might he trip over in the darkness of the hall? Who else had escaped?

The conscious part of his mind was fixed in horror as he watched Louisa rapaciously knotting and tearing and plucking at the silver-gold mass of hair.

"I think I hear your taxi," the old lady said. "Say goodnight, Louisa!"

Louisa said goodnight in her fashion, the door shut behind him—and he was in the car, in the train, in a cold hotel bedroom, with nothing but the letter her mother had written her to remind him that Sarah had ever existed.

Red-Hot Favourite

It was a fatal day for Robert Kellaway, magazine illustrator, confirmed misogynist, and avoider of the female sex when a picture of him appeared in the editorial column of *Herself*.

"All by Herself," the column was called, and the picture of Robert was so very handsome (taken in a lucky moment without his glasses on), the paragraph about his tumbledown old house and bachelor existence in Dulwich was so very chatty, that within a week he had been visited by half the magazine's subscribers and written to by the other half, which, considering that *Herself* had a circulation verging on the million mark, was too much for a man of peaceful and retiring habits. He never wanted to see a pretty face again, or hear a charming voice offering to mend his socks.

Three weeks later he had sold the Dulwich house and was in the bar-parlour of The Goat and Badger in a small village in West Sussex, asking about transport to drag a railway carriage up to the foot of the downs.

"Mr Cowlard would lend you his tractor, daresay," said the landlord, "or Mr Beadle have a pair of carthorses."

"Not horses, no," Robert said, shuddering. "I can't stand the sight of the things. My father used to paint them—Sir Edwin Kellaway, you know, R.A.—and the whole of my childhood was spent giving lumps of sugar to horses to make them stand still in the studio. I'll go and see Mr Cowlard."

Mr Cowlard was willing to oblige, and in the golden evening, when the shadows of the downs lay over the fields like ice-cream cones, an orange-and-blue tractor chugged up the chalky track dragging a second-hand first-class Pullman coach.

Robert had found a secluded spot for his retirement. The abandoned single-track railway from Linfold to Cowchester ran through the downs in a long cutting leading to a tunnel. He had leased half a mile of cutting, and a hundred yards of tunnel to be used as outhouse and spare bedroom. The track had been taken up, so there was no risk of a haphazard express dashing through and spoiling his living arrangements.

It was snug, sheltered, and remote, and Mr Cowlard drove off with the remark that he wished he had a tidy little place like that for when the missis got fratchety.

Food was no problem, since Robert always lived on brown ale, borsch, and breakfast cereals—this had been one of the aspects of his life deplored by *Herself*. He ordered a barrel of beer from The Goat and Badger and brought a gross carton of Oat Crisps with him from London. There was a sugar-beet field below the downs owned by Mr Cowlard, who was glad to exchange some of his crop in return for stories of the wicked goings-on in the magazine world. He often strolled up of an evening with a beet or two and stayed to help Robert convert his Pullman into a studio and drink a peaceful pint over the puzzles on the backs of the Oat Crisp packets. It was an idyllic existence.

Presently Robert remembered that he was nearing the deadline for his next illustration, to accompany a story called "Orchids for Love." He felt strangely unwilling to get going. Firstly he had lost the story—but that was nothing new. He always lost the story, and editors had been known to do damage to the plots of authors from Shaw to Shakespeare sooner than ask Robert to alter his illustrations. The main reason for his reluctance to start, however, was that his glasses had fallen off in the excitement of the move and been crushed under the wheels of Mr Cowlard's tractor, which made him view the world in misty, if beautiful, outline. He had sent the fragments in an Oat Crisp packet to Messrs. Chicory and Flax, opticians in Fleet Street, but had not yet heard from them; it was probable that they were finding the task of repair beyond their powers.

The third obstacle was the difficulty of finding a model who wouldn't start trying to mend his socks.

Robert felt his way down into Linfold, peering about shortsightedly. He gazed with interest at a poster of a handsome black cat on a green background and wondered why it should exhort him to *Keep Albert*. Was Albert the cat? Surely everybody couldn't keep Albert? A few hundred yards farther on it struck him that the poster had probably said *Keep Alert*.

"That's a fine thing to ask a man," he thought dejectedly, and turned into The Goat and Badger to order another barrel of Double Ruby.

"Are there any pretty girls in Linfold?" he asked.

The landlord, who had been so helpful over the transport question, misunderstood him and supplied three addresses in quick succession before Robert managed to explain his needs. Then Mr Cheam shook his head.

"Nary a one in the place; bony as young skeletons with all that horse-riding," he said confidentially.

"I can't abide a horsy woman," Robert agreed.

"Dozens of 'em round here. It's a horsy part of the world. Talkin' of which, can I sell you a ticket for the Derby Sweep?"

"It's a waste of money," sighed Robert, pushing over his half-crown. "I never win anything."

"What 'bout them Oat Crisp puzzles you be forever doin'?" called out Mr Cowlard from farther down the bar. "Wait till 'ee win five thousand from one o' them."

"But talking about women," Mr Cheam went on thoughtfully, "I've got a collection of wigs upstairs; a theatrical lady left 'em behind in settlement of her bill. Would they be any use to you, Mr Kellaway? They say beautiful hair makes all the difference to a pretty face. Put one of them wigs on my Jimmy and he could sit for you as a young lady I daresay."

"That's not a bad idea," Robert agreed. "In fact it's a damn good one."

It was arranged that Jimmy should bring the wigs up that afternoon for a trial sit, and Robert walked back with satisfaction, looking approvingly at the charming wavy village, his eyes misty from myopia and Double Ruby. He read a placard on the smithy relating to the use of garden hoses as *The Use of Career Horses is Strictly Forbidden,* and reflected with vague wonderment on what these animals might be: vicious tuft-hunting beasts, no doubt, who, once getting the bit between their teeth, dashed off in headlong career down the village street—

"Damn," he said, falling over a lump of chalk in the middle of the track. What use could career horses be put to, anyway? Maybe the villagers had laid bets on them until a stern County Council stepped in and said there must be no more of it.

The picture of Jimmy Cheam in a nylon wig, gazing pensively at a bunch of cowslips, was, of course, rather hazy, owing to Robert's lack of glasses.

"Am I really all runny at the edges like that?" said Jimmy. "Coo."

"That's the way I see you," Robert told him severely. "Beauty is in the eye of the beholder." All the same he squinted at the picture doubtfully as he parcelled it up. Larry will just have to make do with it, he said to himself. My glasses should have come by the time the next one's due. Chicory and Flax had sent a postcard regretting their inability to put the splinters together and promising a new pair within six weeks.

In the meantime he embarked on an even mistier picture of Jimmy in an auburn wig with an alice-band of marguerites.

Painting was proceeding some days later when it was interrupted as by a bombshell. A large man bounced into the Pullman, rotund, beaming, carnation-buttonholed—the great Larry Selvage himself, editor of *Herself,* looking with a sort of incredulity first at the clutter around him, then at the white dust on the toes of his beautiful shoes.

"Dear boy! So this is where you have hidden yourself! Don't you find it a little remote? a little rustic? a little rural? Not that it lacks personality of course—wait, and I'll just call up Hawkins from the Cadillac with his camera—"

"No no," cried Robert in agony. "You made Dulwich uninhabitable for me, leave me in peace here, for heaven's sake. When I marry I want it to be from choice, not because I have given up the unequal struggle."

"Very well, very well—" Larry waved a hand soothingly. "Just as you say, dear lad. What I really came to tell you was how breathtakingly appealing your last illustration was—that melting, misty radiance! Marvellous! From now on, nothing but that technique—and we've put your price up by fifty guineas."

"Oh, how—how nice," said Robert weakly. "We must celebrate this. Would you like a plateful of borsch?"

But Larry, giving the Pullman a dismissing glance, preferred to take his chance at The Goat and Badger.

Mr Cheam greeted Robert apologetically. "That's a bit of bad luck your horse has been stolen, Mr Kellaway," he said with sympathy.

"Horse?" Robert was puzzled. "I haven't got a horse."

"Horse you drew in the Derby Sweep," Mr Cheam reminded him. "You had Dog-rose, the favourite, remember? And I see in the paper she've been took and stolen. Still, maybe they'll find her before the race. Police on the track, it says."

"Oh, too bad," Robert said inattentively. "Still, she wouldn't have won if I drew her. I never win anything."

He was soon to be contradicted. When he had seen off Larry in the Cadillac, amid exhortations to keep on painting in his new style, he returned to the Pullman to find two men staring thoughtfully at his piled-up cartons of Oat Crisps. Their faces were a vague blur to Robert, but he could see that they wore bowlers.

"Pretty little spot you've got here, Mr—"

"Kellaway," Robert said, wishing they'd go.

"Undisturbed, eh? Not many strangers?"

"That is why I came here," Robert said pointedly. "I don't expect to see a stranger from one week's end to the next."

"Great eater of Oat Crisps, I see," remarked the smaller bowler. "Ever go in for the competitions?"

"From time to time," Robert admitted.

"I thought so! I knew it! And your first name is—?"

"Robert."

"Not Mr Robert Kellaway?" The little man seemed overwhelmed at his luck. "The very man we've come to find! We have the pleasure of telling you, sir, that you have won a prize in the Oat Crisp contest."

"Five thousand pounds?" asked Robert hopefully.

"No, sir. Better than that—a pure-bred, fully-trained racehorse. We'll bring it up this evening; always better to move a horse after dark, you know, not so unsettling for it."

"But, hey, hold on—" Robert called after their retreating backs, "I don't want a racehorse! I can't stand the blasted things!"

No use; they had gone, and they returned after dusk with a loose box and unloaded a large horse.

"You'll soon get fond of it," they promised, ignoring Robert's protests. "A horse can be a wonderful companion. You'll wonder how you ever did without it." And they departed briskly, even hurriedly, leaving Robert and his new companion face-to-face. Robert reflected with embarrassment and annoyance that he didn't even know the creature's name.

"Here, you, Galloper," he said crossly, "you'd better sleep in the tunnel, you needn't think I'm going to put you up in my studio." And he shoved back the metal-mesh gates.

He did, however, feel obliged to tie a pink eiderdown round the horse's middle, as the tunnel seemed a cheerless sort of bedroom. Then he wondered if the animal had had any supper. Oat Crisps seemed more suitable to offer than borsch, and the horse evidently thought so, too.

"That's enough, that's *enough*, damn it," snapped Robert as Galloper demolished a week's ration. He went to bed in an indignant frame of mind; it was going to be a fine thing if all his extra money from *Herself* was to be spent on the upkeep of a huge, hungry horse.

Next morning, though, looking at Galloper, who proved to be a handsome glossy brown the colour of a horse-chestnut, he couldn't help being rather taken with his new possession. He felt shy about informing the village that he had suddenly joined the despised ranks of horse-owners and decided that, for the time at least, he would keep Galloper's presence a secret, until he and the horse had had a chance to get used to each other. Galloper would have to go into the tunnel when callers were expected.

Later in the day, after ordering another gross of Oat Crisps at the village shop—"How you do get through them, Mr Kellaway," Miss Grooby said—he went into The Goat and Badger to inquire cautiously if there was anybody round about who taught riding.

"Colonel Paragraph," said Mr Cheam at once. "Bottom of the hill, big white house on the right. Can't do better. Thinking of riding in the Derby, Mr Kellaway, ha ha?"

Robert went carefully down the hill. He could now find his shortsighted way through the bumps and crevasses of his own track, but this was strange territory. He began to wonder if he could learn to ride without being able to see more than a couple of yards. Presumably, however, the horse could see where it was going.

He was just able to distinguish the big white house, and went across a cobbled yard where a dimly-glimpsed boy in blue jeans was rubbing down a horse.

"'Morning!" yelled a voice in his ear. He turned and saw a brown-tweeded red peony with a white frill round it: Colonel Paragraph.

"'Morning, sir," said Robert. "I want to learn to ride."

"Couldn't come to a better place," affirmed the Colonel. "Left it rather late, what? Better late than never, though. Soon put you in the way of it. *Phil!*"

"Father?"

"Bring out Daisy and give this young feller an hour's tuition. Same time every morning for three weeks, eh? That suit? Come in after the lesson for a Black Dewdrop and a yarn—always pleased to see a new face."

The boy Phil was friendly and managed to instruct Robert without making him feel too much of a fool; the ride was quite a success. At the end of the hour Phil stabled the horses while Robert went in for his Black Dewdrop, which proved to be a potent mixture of stout and rum.

"M' daughter will be in soon," said the Colonel, but Robert was not at all anxious to meet the Colonel's daughter and quickly took himself off.

The routine of the lessons remained the same, and at the end of three weeks Robert had acquired a fair knowledge of how to sit a horse, had consumed twenty-one Black Dewdrops, and had still managed to avoid meeting the Colonel's daughter.

One evening he decided that it was time to try out his new skill on Galloper, who was frisky as a foal from a steady diet of Oat Crisps and no exercise. Robert put on his saddle and bridle, carefully following Phil's technique, climbed onto Galloper's back from a pile of sleepers, and urged him up the side of the cutting. When they were at the top, and had a clear five miles of downland before them, he gave the horse a tap with a piece of luggage-rack.

The result was electrifying. Galloper did not jerk or bound or gather himself together: he just started. He started into a sort of jet-propelled forward motion that only occasionally brought him in contact with the ground. Bushes, trees, stones, gateposts swung past indistinguishably, and Robert sat tight and prayed. After a bit he began to enjoy it and prayed a little less; this smooth hurtle was pleasingly different from Daisy's bouncing canter. His only worry was, when would it stop?

To his relief, after about twenty minutes Galloper began to slow down a little and Robert was able to turn him round and make for home at a more reasonable pace. All the same it had been quite an experience, and he began to acknowledge that there was something to be said for this riding caper; it was certainly a quick way of getting about the country.

"I have a horse," he said next morning to Phil, "that goes a lot faster than this."

"What sort of horse?" Phil's tone was sceptical. Plainly he didn't trust Robert to know a horse from a camel.

"A racehorse," said Robert. "His name's Galloper. Come up to the Pullman and see him," he added hospitably. It occurred to him that he had now painted Mr Cheam's Jimmy in each of the wigs and it was time he looked out for a new model; this boy appeared to have a harmless sort of muzzy face, what could be seen of it. "Come up this evening."

He tidied Galloper a bit before the professional's visit; polished off stray crumbs of Oat Crisp and gave him a rub with a suede brush. As Galloper blew sociably down his neck, he reflected that it would be quite amusing to paint Phil sitting on the horse; make an interesting bit of composition.

Presently Phil appeared on Daisy with a little parcel bearing the blessed label of Chicory and Flax.

"There's two men with a loose box at the bottom of the hill," he said. "Are you getting another horse? Oh, and the postman asked me to give you this." Then he stopped and gazed openmouthed at Galloper.

"There!" said Robert proudly. "That's a proper racehorse, isn't it?"

"Where did you get her?"

"Won him. Did you say *her?*"

"Well, she's a mare, isn't she? But don't you know what she is? That's Dog-rose, the favourite that was stolen."

"Oh, nonsense," Robert said. "Absolute bosh. How do you know? Horses are all alike, you can't tell one from another like that. His name is Galloper and he answers to it, don't you, Galloper?"

All the same a nasty chilly doubt began to gnaw at his mind. This boy seemed very sure of his facts; he probably studied form, whatever that meant. Supposing those two men in bowlers had stolen Galloper—Dog-rose—this would be an excellent place to leave him hidden while pursuit died down. And then they would come back—

"Hey," he said to Phil. "Did you say there were two men with a loose box?"

"Yes."

"Little men with bowlers?"

"Yes, they did have bowlers."

Robert became inspired. "Now listen," he said. "They are the miscreants who palmed off this valuable racehorse on me under false pretences. But I have a plan. I can hear them coming up now. You must take Galloper through the tunnel, out the other end—the gate's always left open—and gallop over the downs to the police station at Cowchester. I'll hold these chaps in play till you're well away, and if they turn nasty I can retreat into the tunnel too and shut the gate on them. You can leave Daisy inside. Now scram—race-gangs always carry razors, I believe."

In fact they could hear the van toiling up the track, and Phil vanished into the tunnel-mouth with Galloper and was soon out of earshot.

Robert flung himself down in a careless attitude on the turf and began studying an Oat Crisp packet. When the little men appeared, he greeted them gaily.

"Good evening," he said. "Don't tell me I've won another horse? Or have you called in to see how Galloper's getting on?"

He hadn't had time to undo the sealed parcel containing his glasses, so he could not see their expressions.

"I'm afraid an unfortunate mistake has occurred," said Small Bowler. "We have discovered that the award was wrongly made. The horse should have gone to a Mr Oswald Kellaway, and we have come to take it back. Naturally, a written apology from Oat Crisps, Limited, will follow in due course."

"My middle name is Oswald," Robert said affably.

"Now, no joking, please, Mr Kellaway." Small Bowler's tone was curt and cold. "A mistake was made, and we have to rectify it. Where is the horse? I don't want any unpleasantness, but it's a valuable piece of property, and it's coming with us."

"I pawned him," said Robert.

The little man let out a sort of snarl and moved nearer to Robert, who noticed something glinting in his right hand: a piece of horse-equipment, no doubt.

Robert suddenly lost patience. "It's no use your looking for him," he said rashly, "because he's halfway to Cowchester by this time and the police will be looking for *you*, you lousy pair of swindlers."

The object in Small Bowler's hand went off with a loud bang, and Robert's parcel shattered into fragments.

"Look here!" he snapped. "Those were my new glasses."

Then wisdom overtook him, and he leapt into the tunnel entrance, slammed the gate, and raced a hundred yards into the gloom. A couple more bangs behind suggested that the vindictive bowlers were still trying to get him, and bullets ricocheted off the mossgrown concavities of the tunnel. Then they evidently gave it up as a bad job, and he heard the van start and drive off.

"They'll try to intercept Galloper on the way to Cowchester," Robert said to himself, "but it's twenty miles by road and they can't go over the top of the down. They'll never catch him."

Highly satisfied with himself, he mounted Daisy and guided her towards the tiny pinprick of light that was the Cowchester entrance. There was no use in going back, because the gate worked on a spring lock and he kept the key in the Pullman; he would have to continue on and round.

Gradually the pinprick became a keyhole, and expanded to a circle, as Daisy crunched along the permanent way. It grew bigger and bigger, and then Robert began to notice with dismay a metal tracery across it—

"Hullo," hailed a cheerful voice. "I hope you've brought a key with you, because this gate is locked."

"*What?*"

"I suppose they wanted to stop sheep from getting in," said Phil. "We'll have to sneak back and out your end when we're sure those men have gone."

"We'll have to spend the night in the tunnel," corrected Robert gloomily. "Unless you're any good at smashing a lock with a stone."

Unfortunately they couldn't even get at the lock, which was on the far side of the steel mesh. It was the neatest prison ever devised.

"Mr Cowlard might let us out. He comes up to see you in the evenings, doesn't he, sometimes?"

"He's in bed with lumbago."

"Oh. Well, I suppose the postman will let us out in the morning. It's a pity it's so damp and stony in here. Still, we've got Dog-rose, that's the main thing."

"Why the devil did they leave him with me? Do I look like a sucker?"

"They do call you crazy Mr Kellaway in the village because you always look so puzzled," said Phil. He chuckled. "I expect that's what gave the men the idea you'd be a safe bet. And it's nice and secluded."

"I'm not puzzled," said Robert angrily. "I'm shortsighted, that's all. And now those spivs have broken my new pair of glasses. It's all very well for you to laugh, you wretched boy—"

"Say that again," interrupted Phil. Robert patiently repeated what he had said.

"Oh—oh well, of course if you're shortsighted that explains a lot. Do you think," said Phil, "it would be sensible to walk back to your end of the tunnel now?"

"Very well." Robert's tone was chilly. He was wondering how he could make conversation to this boy through the long hours of the night. They started plodding back through the dark with their mounts.

"Do you like cricket?" Robert asked laboriously.

"No," said Phil. But luckily it turned out that Phil was an enthusiastic admirer of Gauguin and Matisse; indeed, Robert had to admit that the boy was an intelligent and amusing companion, and the night passed far more quickly than he would have thought possible. They were stiff and chilly, though, by the time Fred the postman appeared and let them out.

"I suppose I'll have to take Galloper to the police," said Robert sadly when they were drinking coffee in the Pullman.

"I expect there's a reward," Phil consoled him. "You can buy another horse."

That evening, after Robert had paid a rather shamefaced visit to the police with Galloper, and had been mercilessly ribbed in The Goat and Badger for receiving stolen property, he went on to inquire if Phil was all right after his night in the tunnel.

To his surprise, Colonel Paragraph was very indignant.

"I suppose you realize you ought to marry my daughter, young feller?" he barked.

"Your daughter?" said Robert, utterly at sea. "I've never laid eyes on her. You must be thinking of somebody else."

"Never laid eyes on her, he says? Didn't you spend the whole night with her in the tunnel? You've compromised her, sir, compromised her!"

"Don't talk nonsense, Father," said Phil, coming in with two Black Dewdrops. "He didn't even know I was female."

"Wh—what did you say?" stammered Robert hoarsely.

By Derby Day Robert had grown accustomed to his engaged state and was finding it quite enjoyable. He even felt secure enough to submit to Larry Selvage's paragraph beginning: *Handsome Bob Kellaway has been caught at last.* His third pair of glasses had not arrived, so he had painted two hazy, gauzy portraits of Phil sitting on fat Daisy, wearing Mr Cheam's wigs. They had discovered a lot more conversational topics. In fact they would just as soon have stayed at home and gone on painting and talking, but Colonel Paragraph insisted that they must go to the Derby, in which the recovered Dog-rose was a hot favourite.

"If he wins," Robert said, "the manufacturers of Oat Crisps are going to pay me £3,000."

"Should be enough to marry on, my boy, what?" said the Colonel. "Here, you can't see a dam' thing, can you? Have my field-glasses for the run in."

Robert looked through the glasses, but the first thing he saw was his fiancée, Miss Philippa Paragraph, looking so ravishingly beautiful and loving that he felt quite faint. Nemesis had caught up with him at last. He lowered the glasses to reduce her to a bearable haze once more, and stood blissfully holding her hand as Dog-rose romped home to a spectacular finish.

Spur of the Moment

"The radio is out of order," said Mr Newbery, putting his head round the kitchen door. "Would you mind singing?"

It was his peculiarity that he could only work if accompanied by music. Julia obligingly broke into "The First Nowell" as she sprinkled Neap over the breakfast dishes.

Her father lingered a moment or two, straightening the sprigs of holly in the dish-rack, in order to give genius time to kindle. "You ought to let each dish drain for one and three-quarter minutes before drying it," he said reprehendingly.

Julia raised her eyebrows and, without ceasing to sing, reached down a tea-towel printed "Be a Deer and Dry Up." Mr Newbery took the hint and escaped rapidly back to his study.

Just as Julia finished the dishes there was a thunderous banging on the front door, which burst open. A loud voice shouted, "Hullo, 'ullo, 'ullo. Happy Christmas Eve! Anybody at home?"

"Oh lord," Mr Newbery muttered distractedly. "It's that young man of yours. Can't you get rid of him?"

But he heard his treacherous daughter exclaiming in accents of rather overdone surprise and delight, "Why, Hugh! Fancy seeing you so soon after breakfast! You couldn't have come at a better moment; my bike's got a puncture, and Father was just saying the radio's gone wrong."

Hugh came boiling in like the south-west wind, grinning from ear to ear. He had a set of teeth worthy of Red Riding Hood's grandmother, but the disposition behind the teeth was, Mr Newbery privately considered, regrettable: like a houseleek. Hugh had taken hold of the Newberys and put down roots, and was using up more and more space that might have been better employed.

"What do you see in that oaf?" Mr Newbery often lamented to Julia, and she said blandly, "But he's so useful!"

In a twinkling now Hugh had the puncture mended and the radio put to rights, but Mr Newbery doubted if these benefits were worth the lectures on Care of Tyres and Getting the Most out of Your Battery that they were then obliged to sit through.

Julia made coffee. "Not strong enough, Juley," Hugh said. "You ought to put one heaped measure for every cup. Ought to get an espresso machine really, Dad, you know."

"I'm not your Dad yet," said Mr Newbery with restraint.

"Well, well. Won't be long now, as the monkey said when the mower cut his tail off. Come for a run over to Brinsley, Juley? I'm demonstrating efficiency methods there today."

"No, thank you, Hugh," said Julia. "I must clean out the pantry. And there's the turkey to stuff."

"Should come, you know; do you good. Brighten those wits a bit. She's been a bit dull lately, hasn't she, Dad?"

But Mr Newbery said he must get back to his work; if Julia wanted to spring-clean the pantry on Christmas Eve it was her affair. When Hugh had gone, though, he reappeared and said, "Julia, you must shed that incubus. He is slowly sapping what remains of my mind. I can't work any more; I sit in a paralysis of fright waiting for a bang on the door and those shouts of 'Hullo, Dad!' He is too hearty for this degenerate family, Julia; either he goes or you go. But before you go I want some help with my new programme."

"Programme?" said Julia, whose method of spring-cleaning the pantry appeared to consist of sitting on the kitchen table and reading a literary weekly. "But I thought *Town Hat* was the success of all television successes?"

"So it is, so it is," said her father testily. "But we must not rest on our laurels. The trouble is that I'm getting bored with it. I'm utterly stuck for ideas. I need stimulating company. What's the use of a daughter who attracts suitors like flies when all they can do is mend punctures? Put away that snobbish highbrow paper, take this twenty pounds, which is probably our last, go to Rampadges, buy any ten or more articles, and bring them home."

"May I buy clothes?" said Julia, looking suddenly alert.

"No clothes."

"Oh."

"You must buy at random. And be back in time for tea; I want to try to get something sketched out before that repulsive young man turns up again. I'm hoping that your selection of purchases will put some ideas into my head."

Julia bolted upstairs and returned almost immediately in town clothes and a silly but enchanting hat like a lemon with white frills. Mr Newbery looked at her gloomily.

"Don't pick anybody up," he admonished her. "Ten inanimate objects."

"Do I ever?" She flashed him an innocent, speedwell-blue glance and ran from the house.

Richard Stoke usually walked to his office, the firm of Stoke and Pringle, Architects and Surveyors, in which he was slowly qualifying to step into the shoes of Stoke Senior. This morning he was late. He jumped on a bus.

"Upstairs," said the conductor, giving him a martyred look.

It is not easy to achieve complete control of a sextant and a four-foot spirit-level while leading a large and lively Alsatian puppy, but Richard was adept after much practice. Raoul, the puppy, went on ahead while Richard encouraged him from behind with the level.

The conductor, after the manner of his kind, came darting upstairs in pursuit so as to cause Richard the maximum inconvenience by asking for his fare before he had his impedimenta stowed. Luckily there was a diversion: the girl across the aisle had dropped a threepenny piece. Burdened as she was with two large pineapples and, moreover, apparently suffering from hiccups, she was having some difficulty in recovering it.

"I'm so sorry," she apologised sweetly to the conductor. "I always get hiccups if I have to travel on the top deck."

By the time the vanquished conductor had found her coin for her, Richard had produced his own threepence and had fallen in love. When the girl got out at Rampadges, Richard urged Raoul to his feet and followed her like a hypnotic subject.

She darted first to the stationery and book counter, where she bought three sermon pads, reduced to one-and-eleven, and a manual called *How to Build Your Own Cathedral in 100 Man-Hours.* Next she acquired a musical box, and then moved to the electrical department, where she lingered over a display of sunlamps.

A knot of last-minute Christmas shoppers surged by. When they had passed, Richard was disconcerted to see that as well as the sunlamp she was purchasing a deaf aid. Was this enchanting creature deaf?

But sidling closer—as well as he could for Raoul, the sextant, and the spirit-level—he heard her say to the assistant, "Oh, no, it's for my father, the bishop. He gets worried, you know, when he can't hear the cathedral bells, so he's been insisting on ringing the tenor bell himself, and of course that's bad for his tired heart."

The look of grave, daughterly concern on her face was bewitching, Richard thought as he followed her to the sports department, where he was startled to overhear her buying a pogo stick—"For my father, so that he can nip across the Close when he's late for Matins. He's getting rather old and stiff, and this will be a great help."— and an inflatable, rubber paddling pool. "We are going to fill it with Epsom Salts," she explained solemnly to the woman who sold it to her. "Then Daddy needn't go to Tunbridge Wells every April." She also bought two pairs of snowshoes, observing that you never knew when they would come in handy.

As she had by now acquired a largish heap of parcels, she left them all in the travel goods department while she bought a duffel bag to put them in.

Next she made for the Food Hall, whither Richard pursued her—and a kindly assistant gave Raoul a free sample of Puppikrisp. The way led through the pet department; in passing, the girl was seduced by a parrot offered at the bargain price of five pounds.

"It's because he bites, miss," the man told her. "I wouldn't advise you to have him, he can be downright nasty if he takes a dislike to anyone."

"Oh, but that's just what we need at home," the girl explained. "Since the minor canons started their skiffle group, they've given Father no peace: always asking him to join. A bad-tempered parrot in the porch might keep them away."

However, to discourage it from being bad-tempered on the journey home, she paused at the wine counter and bought a miniature bottle of Drambuie, which, administered to the parrot on the spot, soon had it in an amiable and contemplative frame of mind. She also bought a quart of cider and, at the next counter, a large cooked chicken.

Richard wondered if the cider was for the bishop or to maintain the parrot's good humour. He was more and more amazed at the charm and capability of this girl. Imagine being able to keep a shopping list of such length and complexity in one's head! And she had entirely

Joan Aiken

tamed the parrot. It was clambering happily up and down the pogo stick, which she carried like a spear, muttering, "Help, fire! Help, fire!"

She paused now, and carefully counted the change in her purse, hesitated, and finally stopped in the boating department. "How much is that rope?" she asked, pointing to a coil.

"Elevenpence a fathom, miss."

"I can only afford five fathoms. Would that be enough to hang myself?"

"Oh, yes, ample," the young assistant began, and then stopped dead, yardstick in hand, and gasped. "But, madam—"

"Yes," the girl said seriously and sadly, "there's such endless trouble between my father and my boyfriend that I've decided there's only one way to end it all." And she stood with lips folded together, staring straight in front of her like Boadicea, while the shaken young man cut off a length of rope and coiled it, and Richard, equally shaken, wondered with what words he could dissuade this ravishing girl from her dreadful project.

One thing was certain. He must not take his eyes from her. At all costs he must follow her home, in case her father, the bishop, was out conducting Evensong or ringing the tenor bell when she got back. She must not be left on her own for a moment.

He edged after her through the parcel-laden crowds.

Two hours and several nightmarish bus rides later, Richard was still gamely in pursuit. They were in the wilds of Surrey, it had begun to snow—"Those snowshoes will come in handy," Richard thought parenthetically—and both Raoul's and Richard's stomachs were protesting that lunch was long overdue, and there seemed little reason to believe that tea would not be likewise. The conductor, two old ladies, Richard, Raoul, the parrot, and the girl were the only passengers remaining. The bus was toiling up a steep and tree-girt incline.

80

The old ladies rang the bell, and the bus came to a slithering stop.

When, after they had alighted, the driver tried to start again, there was a frenzied noise of racing engine but no movement.

"He's done it again," the conductor said resignedly. "I told him not to stop on this hill when there's snow, but he always forgets. Would you mind getting out and helping me push, ladies and gents, please? The luggage can stay inside."

This Julia interpreted to mean the parrot, the pogo stick, and her duffel bag, while Richard left his sextant and spirit-level, now registering an acute variation from the horizontal. They walked to the back of the bus and looked at it without enthusiasm, as it tilted over them like some cornice in the frosty Caucasus. Snowflakes pouring down thick as butterflies silted on Julia's frivolous hat and made Raoul sneeze.

"When I wave my hand, push," called the driver.

"Raoul, come here," said Richard.

"Why do you call him Raoul?" asked Julia, getting ready to push.

The driver waved his hand and they struggled and shoved like coal-heavers.

"After the Vicomte de Bragelonne," panted Richard. "He was the son of Athos, you remember. He was jilted by Louise de la Vallière."

"And has Raoul been jilted?" gasped Julia, much interested. The bus was beginning to move.

"Not that I—puff—know of, but the name sounds like the noise"—they were both running now, and the bus was grinding along—"that he makes when I leave him behind." And indeed Raoul raised his voice in a long, lamentable howl and came loping after them. "He can't bear being left." Keep her mind occupied, he thought, that's the way. "You see, I used to work for a firm of cookery-book publishers, making up cocktail recipes. I had to drink forty to eighty cocktails a day. Quite against my will I was turning into a dipsomaniac."

Raoul caught them up, and the bus, with a terrific roar of acceleration, spurted away over the crest of the hill and left them.

"I do hope the driver will remember we're not on board," said Julia. "But how do the cocktails tie up with Raoul?"

"I'm coming to that. My Aunt Adelaide was worried about me, and when she died she left me Raoul with instructions that I was to take him everywhere. She knew that meant I'd have to change my job and get something in the open air. Thanks to her I'm now completely cured."

"So you could get rid of Raoul now?"

"She said I was never to part with him unless I could find him a home in a bishop's family."

Julia darted an acute, blindingly blue glance at him, but he was staring innocently ahead through the snow. "Look, there's our bus waiting," he said.

The journey was resumed, but soon Richard saw that Julia was getting ready to descend. She wound the parrot's chain firmly round the pogo stick and shouldered her duffel bag. He picked up the spirit-level.

"Is this your stop, too?" asked Julia with a certain suspicion.

"I'm taking observations and collecting statistics regarding the height and distribution of pine trees in Surrey," Richard replied promptly. "The Comet Film Corporation, a small British company, is making a film of *Lohengrin* and they want Teutonic-looking scenery for the outside shots. Of course, it's unfortunate that the pines in Surrey are nearly all *p. sylvestris,* but I daresay they'll be able to make do."

"Not very good weather for making a survey, surely?" said Julia. She stopped, sat in the snow under a bush, and strapped on a pair of snowshoes. "Would you care to borrow a pair?"

"Thank you; I would like to very much. Beggars can't be choosers," said Richard in a melancholy tone. "If I don't somehow get some money to pay my rent, Raoul and I will be sleeping in the crypt of St. Martin's-in-the-Fields." He finished lacing his snowshoes, stood up, and shouldered her duffel bag.

"That's very kind of you," Julia said uncertainly. They plodded on through the snow together and presently came within sight of a small cottage.

"Isn't there a cathedral around here?" said Richard casually.

"Not nearer than Guildford. Why do you ask?"

"The spire would have been useful for taking an elevation. Never mind, I can manage without." But it was now his turn to survey her with suspicion as she unlatched the garden gate.

Meanwhile Hugh had returned from his demonstration. At four o'clock he dropped artlessly round to the Newberys'. "Any tea going, Juley?" he bawled.

No answer. He poked his head through the kitchen door, saw a kettle on the floor and, looking round the corner of the entrance, found Mr Newbery irritably winding a well-handle. It was a peculiarity of the cottage that the well was in the scullery.

"Now, now, now, Dad," said Hugh, sliding his cigarette farther into the corner of his mouth and advancing on Mr Newbery, who would have bolted had there been another door. "Pump's not gone wrong since I mended it, surely?"

"Bit slow in starting," mumbled Mr Newbery, who had long since found it simpler to wind himself up a bucket of water as required than engage in the hellish pump-starting routine.

"*I'll* finish winding and then I'll start her up for you," said Hugh, chivalrously wrenching the handle away from him. He gave it a tremendous jerk, the aged rope broke, and the bucket dropped back into the well with a splashing clatter.

"*Now* look what you've done," snarled Mr Newbery, at the end of his tether. "All I want is one cup of tea, and a chance to drink it in peace and quiet. What a hope! Not a drop of water in the house, and rugger-playing oafs in and out all day long."

"Soccer, not rugger," said Hugh, not a bit discomposed. "Y'know, Dad, you keep this pump in a shocking condition. Tank's empty, too. No wonder she won't go." He strode out and returned with a can. Mr Newbery was feverishly looking in all the empty milk-bottles, vases, or jugs which might conceivably hold water and finding none.

"How much does she hold?" Hugh asked, after he had put in some petrol. "Got a torch?"

"Battery's run out."

"Always ought to keep a spare in the house." Casually Hugh lit a match and peered into the petrol tank. There was a small but brisk explosion. A tongue of flame shot out, annihilated Julia's nylons on a towel-horse, and leapt to a pile of potato-sacks.

"I told you so," said Mr Newbery rather unfairly. He shrugged his shoulders and retired to the kitchen. Julia and Richard were just coming in. He looked at Richard balefully. "Your other young man," he said to Julia, "has set fire to the house. The well-rope's broken, the bucket's down at the bottom. It's a pity I forgot to pay the insurance."

Hugh came rushing out. "It's hopeless," he gasped. "Get out while you can!" He himself set the example.

Richard wandered to the scullery door. "Have you a telephone?" he said.

"The Exchange always takes twenty minutes to answer," Julia murmured regretfully, indicating the instrument.

Richard linked the parrot's chain round the flex and took off the receiver. Then he emptied out the contents of the duffel bag and gave the bird a tot of cider. It perched obediently on the receiver and began shouting, "Help, fire! Help, fire!"

"Someone will hear that sooner or later," said Richard. "Now"— he was tying one end of the coil of rope to the mouth of the duffel bag—"if you, Your Grace, will inflate that paddling pool"—He handed Mr Newbery the pump off Julia's bicycle—"and you"—he passed Julia his snowshoes—"could wrap these in a wet tea-cloth and beat out the smouldering bits of the fire."

He swung his improvised bucket down the well, brought it up full, and tossed the contents over the blazing sacks. Before drawing a second bucketful he reached down into the well with the pogo stick, hooked up the rightful bucket, and emptied it into the paddling pool which Mr Newbery had now inflated. "This will do as a reservoir, since two people can't draw water at the same time." He passed Mr Newbery the bucket and drew out six more duffel bags full.

"Ingenious," said Mr Newbery admiringly. He emptied half his bucketful on the fire, reflected a moment, poured the rest into the kettle, and put it on the range in the kitchen. Then he went back to his task. The fire was almost out by now, and after a few more bucketfuls he decided that he could make tea and leave the rest to Julia and the new young man.

"Help, fire!" shouted the parrot for the hundred and fiftieth time. It glared beadily at Raoul by the range and launched itself at him like a dive-bomber. The telephone fell off the windowsill and dangled quacking at the end of its flex.

"It's all right, thank you, the fire's out," Mr Newbery said politely into the receiver before replacing it.

Raoul had taken refuge with his master, so the parrot, cheated of its prey, turned on Hugh, who had just reappeared with a stirrup-pump. "Now you'll be all right," he was shouting. The parrot pecked him.

"Oh, go and take a running jump at yourself, you and your efficiency methods," Mr Newbery snapped.

Julia and Richard emerged, black, damp, and triumphant. "Rather busy just now, Hugh," Julia said absently. "I'm going to clean out the pantry."

"If I get psittacosis I shall sue you," Hugh said angrily. Even he could see he was not wanted.

Mr Newbery picked up, *How to Build Your Own Cathedral.* "Here, dear boy," he said. "With the compliments of the season." And, as Hugh left, slamming the door, he added, "Let's hope that's the last we shall see of him for a hundred man-hours."

The door shot open again and two brawny and beaming firemen dashed in. "All right, Mr Newbery," shouted one of them. "We'll soon have her out. Where's the trouble?" They quested about like bloodhounds.

"Oh, not more efficiency experts," sighed Mr Newbery ungratefully.

"Sorry not to get here sooner," the larger fireman apologised when they were really convinced there was nothing to be done and were drinking cups of tea. "Miss Mumpsey at the Exchange is that deaf it's a wonder she puts through any calls at all. Matter of fact we were down there having a bit of a warm-up—the Fire Station's so cold—and that's how we came to hear of your little blaze."

"It was most kind of you, most kind," said Mr Newbery with distinguished courtesy. "A little token of seasonal good will"—he fished about in the clutter on the kitchen table and extracted the sun-lamp—"to warm up the Fire Station, and perhaps you would call in with this present for Miss Mumpsey on your way back? I am told these appliances improve one's hearing marvellously. A happy Christmas to you!"

Beaming, the firemen withdrew. "As for this young man who has helped us with such a genius for improvisation"—Mr Newbery turned cordially to Richard—"we must reward him, Julia, to the best of our ability."

He delved again on the kitchen table. "Would you, my dear fellow, prefer a sextant, a spirit-level, a pogo stick, or a paddling pool? The parrot, I perceive, has left us already."

"It's very kind of Your Grace," Richard began, but Julia cut in.

"What about the programme, Father—if you go giving everything away?"

"It has already taken root in my mind," Mr Newbery said happily. He wound up the musical box, and it began to play "The First Nowell" in the breathless tinkle common to such instruments. He handed it to Richard and picked up the sermon pads. "I'm going to retire and rough it out now. It will be called *Spur of the Moment.* Two people, a heap of miscellaneous objects, a crisis—yes, yes. Get rid of your young friend, Julia, and you can type for me. I fear the buses will have stopped running, but it is only five miles to the station and the snow is not more than eight inches deep."

"I'm afraid I suffer from snow-blindness," said Richard decisively. "In that respect I take after my grandfather, who walked round and round Trafalgar Square and eventually died of exposure. There's not a hope that I should survive the walk."

"In that case you must of course stay the night," said Mr Newbery, capitulating with grace and the respect due to a fellow-improviser. "You won't object to sleeping in the paddling pool? Perhaps you might help me with my TV programme?"

"TV," said Richard. The last piece of the jigsaw fell into place.

"I will join you both for dinner at eight," said Mr Newbery benevolently. He waved his sermon pads at them and withdrew. Raoul snored peacefully by the glowing grate.

"He's so comfortable here, it's a pity this isn't a bishop's family," said Julia thoughtfully. "Oh, by the way, hadn't you better ring Comet Films and tell them you're snowbound?"

"Ahem," said Richard. "As to that . . ." He grinned. Julia, standing with a pineapple under each arm, grinned back.

"Perhaps we'd both better begin at the very beginning," she suggested.

The Paper Queen

The town of Rohun, or Rune, was a dying town, and its inhabitants liked it that way. They liked the gravel shoal in the river below the twelve-arched bridge that stopped paper barges coming up to the wharfside any more. They liked the gentle air of ruin in the church square, the dead quiet that listened to its own breathing of a Sunday, the fact that there wasn't a fishmonger's nearer than St. Malpus, to which the bus ran only in the summer.

Old as it was, and full of legends, the town was able to dispense with most of them. A legend is how granny made the tea with linseed oil the day her spectacles fell into the separator, and no one in their senses bothers to keep alive a lot of dead old tradition when tradition is building itself up all the time, like the gravel shoal in the River Rune.

Porteous Snawl meant to change all this. When he first came to the town he saw that it had possibilities as a summer resort, and in less than no time he had grown a black beard, so as to look like a retired sea captain, and started up a sweet-and-mineral shop, hiring out motorboats to visitors in the summer and transforming his bit of cobbled yard into a tea garden.

By his second year he was on the water board, housing committee, and library suggestion panel, and in three years he was mayor. The River Rune had been cleared so that paper barges could once more proceed up river to the Merlinhay Mills, water was laid on in some of the council houses, and some of their windows were mended, too, and there was talk of buying new books for the library.

And were the natives pleased? They were a peaceful crew, the people of Rune; in actual fact they hardly noticed the ant-like activity of Mr Snawl, though they did see that his daughter Helen was more than commonly pretty. In their own way they too were busy: fishing for salmon in the Rune River before dawn of a July morning, singing the *Messiah* in the leafy, smoky autumn twilight, scratching the backs of each others' lean pigs in the springtime.

Only one thing was of importance to them, and this was the band-playing. On Christmas Eve the town's four silver bands wandered about the streets from daybreak till well after dark, playing carols. Let Mayor Snawl revive, if he would, the decayed Regatta, the crowning of the Paper Queen, the Gorsedd of local poets on a hilltop recently rechristened Arthur's Throne, and the townspeople had no objection, as long as no one interfered with the bands.

Christmas Eve is a grand time to come out of prison if you have a loving, family warming your stockings and making your mince pies. Young Mark Pentecost had no family because his mother had died when he was born and his father was drowned in the flood of thirty-seven when Fore Street was eighteen feet deep and the church swam on the water like a Noah's Ark.

When Mark came out of St. Malpus' jail, therefore, he strolled across the moors with no particular goal in mind. The whole world was misty and frosty as a dream, and tendrils of smoke from the chimneys of Rune were uncurling among the early stars as he came down Market Street. Far and near the soft tidings of the bands soared up into the dusk so that shoppers buying celery at the greengrocer's were reminded of "The First Nowell," and moved on round the corner to

"Good King Wenceslas" at the butcher's, while the lending library was filled with "The Holly and The Ivy."

Mark went to the Dolphin. It was not opening time yet but Bill Pettigrew, the landlord, who was a friend and had been looking after his barge while he was in prison, gave him a cup of tea in the kitchen and told him the gossip.

"He's certainly buttered his paws," said Bill (they were talking of Mr Snawl). Managing director of the paper mills he is now, and running for Parliament at the next election. Though why run? He'd get in just as fast by standing."

Bill laughed his round, barrel-like laugh, and after a while Mark laughed, too.

"So, what did you do in prison?" Bill asked presently, bringing out a pair of little crystal glasses, for tea without sloe gin is like a canoe without a paddle.

"Learnt to read," said Mark bitterly. "Think of it! Me! A Pentecost! What I don't know about boats and pigs they could tie up in a daisy leaf and hide in a mouse's ear, and they have to teach me to *read*! Every day I had to write out: 'I must not sell the mayor poached salmon on Good Friday, I must not box with the mayor's son on Easter Saturday, and I must definitely not kiss the mayor's daughter on Easter Sunday.'"

"Handsome!" said Bill with admiration. "They'm grand places, these reform schools. Fed and clothed for three years, and education into the bargain. *And* back in time for the crowning of the Paper Queen."

"Paper Queen?" said Mark. "My barge?" He was out of touch with local doings.

"No, no. 'Tis the old ancient custom, the mayor's been reviving, with a crowning and a paper fight and procession through the streets of Rune. Proper fine queen she'll make, too."

"Who?"

"Why, she. Helen. The Mayor's daughter."

Mark was digesting this when he noticed that old Mr Santo, Bill Pettigrew's father-in-law, who had been sitting the other side of the hearth all this time, was crying quietly into his teacup, the tears streaming silently down his whiskery old face.

"What's the matter, Dad?" he asked, putting down his own cup and getting up to pat the old man's shoulder. "Tea too hot?"

"It's not that." Bill, shaking his head, answered for Mr Santo. "Mayor's moving into his new house today."

"Well?"

"Taken over Hearken House, he has."

"But it's falling to bits."

"He's mended it all to rights, and he'm moving in this evening, time for Christmas."

Mark stared at him with a troubled expression. Hearken House or the Monks' house, as some called it, was an aged gothic building just across the road from the church. No one had lived in it for many years, and it was pretty well derelict. One of its rooms was open to the public. A flight of outside stairs led up to this room, and at the foot of them was a notice that said: "Room available for meditation, prayer, and hearkening." Hence the name of the house. No one bothered to go and hearken in the room except old Mr Santo, and it had been his Christmas Eve habit for many years now to go up and hearken for the voice of dead Mrs Santo. He had never heard it yet, but this in no way detracted from the importance of the ritual.

"Won't he let you hearken?" Mark asked hotly. Old Mr Santo sobbed into his tea, and Bill laced it generously with sloe gin. The old man took a gulp and made some reply, which was drowned in the muted chords of "Hark the Herald," as the station band softly played themselves by, on their way to open the level-crossing gates for the Paddington express.

Bill shook his head sadly. "Couldn't pluck up the courage to ask," he said.

"There's too many things wrong round here," exclaimed Mark, jumping to his feet. "This town's going to rack and ruin, I can see with all these fal-lals and meddling. It's time someone began to put things to rights."

"Where are you off to?"

"Going to find the mayor," Mark shouted, half outside the door already. But in the street he met an obstruction, for a procession was winding its way from Cromwell's steps to the Memorial Hall, and the only thing he could do was fall in with it. Paper streamers flew and snapped, paper snakes flipped in and out, paper whistles were blown, paper hats were worn. It was the coronation procession of the Paper Queen. And there she sat, enthroned in the midst, wearing a dress of white silk stiff and reverent as parchment, her yellow hair the pallor of a Christmas rose, Helen, the mayor's daughter. Mark followed like one in a dream.

In the Memorial Hall the coronation ceremony took place. Various directors of the mills gave Helen this and that scroll, seal, papier-mache sceptre and laminated orb; then her father, grave and dignified down every inch of his four foot ten, placed the crown on her head and proclaimed her Paper Queen of Rune, River, and Polchippery. Everybody cheered.

"Now," said the mayor, when that was done, "every queen has a right to choose her consort, and the Paper Queen has a particular right. Look round the hall, my dear, and pick the man of all men you'd most like to receive a letter from."

Long she looked, and the young men blushed and fidgeted as her cool eye took them in and passed on.

She met Mark's tortured eyes and for a heartbeat-space longer than the whole of the nineteenth century their gaze clung and grappled. Then she turned to an elderly alderman beside her and gave him the ceremonial quill.

"Mr Mutton!" she said. "I'd love to have a letter from you, Mr Mutton." Amid thunderous applause and laughter Mr Mutton climbed onto the second throne and the dancing began.

Mark fought his way round the walls till he reached Mr Snawl. The mayor, laughing with some cronies, had his back to Mark and didn't see him.

"So I've wired an extension speaker into the Hearkening Room," he was saying, "and if old Mr Santo doesn't have a reward for his patience this Christmas, my name's not Porteous Snawl. And that reminds me, Sam, my boy," he added to his son, who was standing nearby, "just run up to the Dolphin, will you, and tell old Santo it's all right for him to come and hearken this evening. He never asked me about it. And don't you stay drinking at the Dolphin," he shouted after Sam, "young Pentecost comes out today, and I don't want you both drunk and disorderly at midnight."

Mark had heard enough. He turned and dived through the crowd in pursuit of Sam, but it was a slow business, and by the time he caught up with the boy he had come out of the Dolphin, his message delivered.

"It's an outrage," Mark said, taking him by the lapel.

"Hey there, Mark! Glad to be out? What's an outrage?"

"Putting an extension speaker in the Hearkening Room. Fooling old Mr Santo."

Sam shrugged. "Father didn't mean any harm. He thinks it's a kindness to the poor old boy, listening away Christmas after Christmas like he does, all for nothing."

"I'm going to stop it." Mark turned back into the Dolphin. People were trickling away from the Crowning and going into the bar. He ran unmolested up the dark stairs, which smelt of dry-rot, down a passage, and into one of the bedrooms.

Sam was hard on his heels. "Anything for a lark," he said, grinning.

Mark flung open a dormer window and hung out, sniffing air like iced champagne—and looking at the vista of silvery roofs. He climbed onto the sill, clutched the roof above him, his fingers digging into the frosty tiles, and kneed himself round into the angle of the dormer. In a moment he was astride the window ridge; in another he was toe-and-fingering his way up the slope of the roof. A tile behind him slipped out and tinkled merrily down to the pavement below. When he was astride the rooftree he turned to see young Sam coming doggedly after him.

"For heaven's sake! You'll be killed."

"No more than you," Sam said, blowing on his numb fingers. "Go on. We can't go back."

Faint and sad the noise of "Once in Royal David's City" came floating up from a strolling band. Another tile, dislodged by Sam, skittered into its midst, and a trombone played a wrong note. Mark set off along the roof ridge.

Hearken House was twelve along from the Dolphin, and many an awkward climb and even more awkward drop faced them as they struggled from one aged, irregular house to another.

"Attic window," said Sam at last, puffing a little.

It was locked, of course. Mark took his shoes from round his neck and broke the window with a heel. They dropped inside and made their way softly down a ladder in the velvet dark. In this house the smell of dry rot had been replaced by that of turps, sawdust, and emulsion paint.

"This way," Sam said.

A huge oblong of moonlight lay like a tablecloth on the bare boards of the Hearkening Room. It was utterly silent: not so much as a farthing's worth of mouse stirring.

"I'm going to cut the wire," whispered Mark. "Where's the speaker?"

Sam began to point, but they were too late. They heard shuffling footsteps, and Sam urgently tugged Mark into the shadow of a cupboard. In came old Mr Santo by the outside door, and Mr Snawl with him, full of solicitude.

"You sit there, Mr Santo; you prefer it dark, don't you? Now I'll leave you. Please make yourself at home and stay just as long as you like. There'll be cake and cider downstairs whenever you want to come down and join us; my daughter is just back from the Crowning. She'll be delighted to see you." He tituped out, and as he passed the door Mark heard a click. Then there was a silence again, deep and thick as a tub of tar, while Mark counted a hundred. What should he do? He started moving, but Sam tugged his hand.

A gentle voice began to sing.

One of the bands was passing by outside, and "O Come All Ye Faithful" for a moment softly filled the room, then faded again, and the voice took over.

"*O the holly bears a blossom as white as the silk*" it sang, and they heard old Mr Santo gasp and catch his breath.

"*And the first tree in the greenwood it is the holly . . .*"

The old man stood up in the moonlight, looking bewildered, and Mark was angry—angrier than he had ever been. Then, suddenly, as he was about to shake off Sam's restraining hand and stride forth, there was another click, the singing stopped, and all the street lamps went out.

"Power failure," breathed Sam at Mark's elbow. "That settles it."

A great flood of relief poured into Mark's mind. All was well. Mr Santo was not going to be fooled. And he himself could go back to the Dolphin and sleep off the great weariness that had overtaken him.

Mr Santo was creaking towards the door when a voice directly overhead made him pause.

"Arthur," it said, acidly.

"Yes, Maria?"

"You go right home this minute. The idea of it! A man your age out at this time on a winter's night! And change your vest when you get home."

"Yes, Maria."

"And go straight to bed. Of all the awkward, troublesome, good-for-nothing husbands, you are the very worst! If I didn't keep after you all the time I don't know what would happen."

"No, Maria."

"And don't go eating any of that nasty, heavy pudding tomorrow."

"No, Maria."

"Happy Christmas!" the voice added as a parting shot.

"Happy Christmas, Maria," old Mr Santo said happily, and he felt his way to the door. The two young men followed him after a moment or two.

Downstairs the mayor's house-warming party was in full swing, lit by candles on account of the power failure.

Mr Santo was in the midst of a long, excited recital to Porteous Snawl, who had a puzzled look.

"You heard a voice? But didn't it stop short in the middle?"

"Oh, no," Mr Santo said blissfully. "First there was a bit of singing, angels maybe, and then she came on herself, her very own voice. I'd know Maria anywhere, though I haven't heard her for thirty years. I must go home and tell Bill and Mary. Oh, thank you, thank you, Mr Snawl, I don't know how to thank you."

Scratching his head, quite at a loss, Mr Snawl turned and saw Mark.

"Oh, you're there," he said affably. "Have a nice time in jail?"

Mark looked at him, in a bitter silence, and began making his way to the door in the wake of old Santo. Just by the entrance he came face-to-face with Helen.

"You!" he said harshly. "Where's your bit of mutton fat?"

"Oh, Mark! Don't be so mean! What was the use of picking you as the man I'd like to get a letter from when I know perfectly well you can't write?"

Mark looked at her, and as this simple explanation dawned on him an expression of great wonder and joy lit up his face. But all he said was, "That's all you know." And pulling from his pocket a bit of paper and stub of pencil he laboriously printed on it, "Mark Pentecost loves Helen Snawl."

"Helen Pentecost is a much nicer name," said Helen dreamily.

"Ah, that's right," exclaimed her father, coming up and seeing what was afoot. "I've a job for you, Mark, in the Works and Planning Department, now you can read and write. I knew the only way to make you learn was to get you jailed for three years. You'll leave that leaky old barge, my boy, and you and I will do big things together: you're the only citizen in this town that has an appreciation of what ought to be done. We'll get the sewers seen to; no more floods; and the roads mended and the bridge widened. I'll see you about it all on Boxing Day."

He nodded graciously to the young couple and bustled off on his mayoral and hostly duties. Mark and Helen went out and strolled dreamily in and out of the decaying, moonlit streets while the current of legend flowed, leaving its silt on the doorsteps and pavements of Rune. Somewhere, not far off, a silver band was playing:

O little town of Bethlehem, how still we see thee lie;
Above thy deep and dreamless sleep the silent stars go by . . .

Octopi in the Sky

ot night. The stars in the velvet sky burnt like sparks on a railway embankment; any moment, it seemed, the whole firmament would be ablaze. The young man, Denis Cobbleigh, lay wretched and sleepless on his luxurious bed; he had flung off the sheets, but the humid dark wrapped him like a cocoon; he had turned off the lights, but the red sky of London glared remorselessly at him through the window.

From where he lay in his Mayfair room, he could see, high over Piccadilly Circus at the top of a builders' construction tower, one of the creations of his fancy, an electric octopus that spun in a never-ending glittering cartwheel, throwing off cascades of light. Each tentacle held a brimming, foam-topped glass of stout.

And underneath, in fiery pink italics, the legend ran (but from where he lay this at least the young man could not see):

For a fast lap—drink Cobbleigh's Cream Stout

Although he shut his eyes he could see it in imagination. He could see, too, its predecessors—the giant squid in the foam-girt saucer announcing "Every Octopuss prefers Cobbleigh's Cream," or the eightsome reel of octopi holding sixty-four bottles aloft and declaring "One over the eight? Never, when it's Cobbleigh's Cream."

Denis shuddered. He knew that these nightmare visions of his, translated into posters, into twenty-times-larger-than-life papier-mache figures, were abroad all over London. This was the reason why he stayed in and kept his eyes shut.

But that was not the worst of it. He knew, as well, that if he opened his eyes and looked steadily into the corner of the room he would see an enormous glass of Cobbleigh's Cream Stout, darker than treacle, its beaded, crusted froth brown as an ear of barley. By the window would be a man-high tankard of ale, and regarding him mournfully over the top a pair of huge cephalopod eyes, sadder than a spaniel's, begging for a drink.

If he dropped his hand by the side of the bed, like as not he would feel an ingratiating molluscular back rising to rub it . . .

> I love little Octo, his coat is so tough
> His taste's so discerning, he knows the right stuff
> I'll give him eight glasses of Cobbleigh's Cream Stout
> And Pussy will love me . . .

"No!" said Denis. And opened his eyes. Above the tankard, above the beaker, the mournful eyes regarded him.

Give us a drink. Please give us a drink! they begged.

"It's no use!" Denis cried despairingly. "If I could, do you think I wouldn't myself?" He dropped his hand. It missed the bedside table, and a smooth curved back rose and rubbed hopefully against it. Angrily Denis snatched up Uncle Dion's bottle of sleeping tablets.

"If you can't sleep, dear boy, take one of these," his uncle had said, months ago. Every night he took one, but they never put him to sleep. He turned and buried his head in the pillow, to shut out the reproachful luminous eyes, and tried to compose a sonnet.

> Greet your green love upon the candled shore . . .

But he could go no further than the first line. Try as he would, his thoughts turned to his uncle, to his uncle's mission the next day in Portsbourne, and without volition his mind began to run in another direction, and to form lines:

Drinking "Tio Pepe,"
Thinking about Rose,
That's the way the evening
Generally goes:
Seven, put the cat out,
Eight, make the tea,
Nine, do the crossword
Or peer at ITV . . .

Irritably he rolled over, kicking the vestigial bedclothes onto the floor. "You won't like sherry!" he threw at the attendant octopi. "It'll make you liverish." And he buried his head again.

Next morning Denis, pale, feverish, but determined, was visiting a psychiatrist. His uncle was out of the way in Portsbourne; it was a golden opportunity.

"You can't sleep?" said Dr. Finlay. He spoke as if it was no great matter.

"I haven't slept for twenty years," Denis explained. "I get all my best ideas at night."

"Your best ideas?"

"Advertising gimmicks," Denis said gloomily. "I'm in charge of the publicity for Cobbleigh's Cream Stout."

"Ah yes—'Drink Cobbleigh's and you're squids in.'"

"I'm beginning to be haunted by squids." Denis glanced at the floor. A small cephalopod rose from the hearth rug where it had been lying and rubbed insinuatingly against the table leg. Dr. Finlay's eyes followed.

"Do you see it, too?"

"A simple case of hypnotism." The psychiatrist's tone brushed this aside. He opened the door, called "Puss! Octopuss!" and gently put the creature outside. "You had better change your occupation."

"Oh, I couldn't possibly do that. It's my uncle's business; I'm the junior partner."

"Sell out."

"Impossible. I owe my uncle a debt of gratitude."

"Why?"

"He saved my life when I was four. He pulled me out of a vat of stout."

"Do you remember the episode?"

"Only dimly," said Denis, shuddering. "I remember a desperate struggle in dark depths; I've been unable to drink stout since that day."

"No wonder," said the psychiatrist with satisfaction. "Very traumatic. We must uncover the whole episode; lay bare its foundations. Come to me every day at ten."

The receptionist showed Denis out. His octopus was waiting for him on the landing, twining itself affectionately on the banisters.

Meanwhile his uncle, three hundred miles away, was being met by a beautiful girl at Portsbourne station.

"Miss Rosita Jerez? How delightful to see you, my dear," he said, beaming, giving an enormous tip to the restaurant car attendant.

"Oh yes, you can *see* me," Rosita said sullenly. "You can *see* me, but you can't talk to me. Mother won't allow it." She looked as if she did not much care either way.

She slammed the rear door on Mr Dionysius Cobbleigh and his briefcase, climbed into the driver's seat, and jerked the big, ugly, shiny car into motion as if she hated it. She herself, Mr Cobbleigh reflected blandly, was not unlike the car: big, angular, expensive, and looked as if she had a fast turn of speed.

"Interesting how these old Spanish customs linger on, even after several generations in England," he murmured to himself—Rosita was taking no notice of him—and he looked out approvingly at the grandeur of the wild view as they ascended the tree-hung flanks of the gorge.

Far downstream a suspension bridge hung twinkling and spindling in the last gold of the sun. It was a most superior place; a *highclass* place, Mr Cobbleigh said to himself, suitable for the deal he had come to make.

He smoothed his white hair and leaned back smiling like an evil old saint, silky as an olive-stone, while they entered a pair of high iron gates and drew up before a white Spanish-style house all embowered in trees. Good, very good. A poker-faced majordomo; girl brought up in true Spanish seclusion; the blood of hidalgos; all very good. A long, long way from the dead cats floating in the waters of the Liffey.

"I will escort you to your room," the majordomo announced. "The Señora will see you in half an hour." Rosita had disappeared.

Cobbleigh grinned to himself. This deal was very unlike his last, fifty years ago, when with the purchase of two rainwater barrels and a heap of barley he had started Cobbleigh's Cream Stout on its epoch-making way. Now he was a millionaire several times over, and was on the lookout for tone.

"The Señora is ready for you."

Mr Cobbleigh followed to a big shadowed room. Venetian blinds and cascades of roses held away the light; all he could see was a black lace mantilla and a pair of very sharp eyes. He prepared himself, with relish, for a hard bit of bargaining.

"So, Mr Cobbleigh," she said dryly, after the formalities had been observed, "you want to buy my business. You want to buy my Avon Gold."

"Very fine stuff, ma'am," said Mr Cobbleigh, turning the delicate glass in his hand. As a matter of fact he did not care for sherry, but it was his business to know quality when he met it. And there was quality here, all right—in this big shady house, in the well-covered girl who had driven him from the station, in the bony, aristocratic face opposite him, in the aromatic drink he held.

"And the figure you were suggesting . . . ?"

He suggested it again. The hard black eyes held a touch of derision.

"It's a failing market, ma'am," said Mr Cobbleigh, who let neither Irish blarney nor Spanish pride stand in his way when coming down to brass tacks. "And you're—pardon me—getting on. Who inherits when you—?"

"That, Mr Cobbleigh," said the Señora, "was why I wanted to see you personally. You have a junior partner, I believe?"

"My nephew."

"A brilliant young man. Your successor, yes?"

"Oh, the boy's a genius after his fashion," Mr Cobbleigh said airily. "He's by way of being a poet." His Irishness came out strong on this word, which he pronounced, with some scorn, as phoo-ut.

The Señora nodded, satisfied. "You met my daughter, yes?" Mr Cobbleigh's eyes gleamed. He began to see whither they were tending.

"A handsome girl. An heiress. No expense spared over her education. Private tuition in hockey and polo, to fit her for an English husband. Now she lives in strict seclusion, as befits a young Spanish lady of high family. Nevertheless we have been beset by fortune hunters. I have had my hands too full with keeping them at bay to manage the business properly. I wish her to be suitably settled."

Mr Cobbleigh nodded.

"Now, your nephew, Mr Cobbleigh—I might see my way to accepting your *perfunctory* figure for the ancient and noble house of Jerez's Avon Gold if your nephew—"

Mr Cobbleigh rose. He bowed. "Say no more, ma'am. The take-over's as good as completed. We might try mixing 'em—Cobbleigh's Cobbler, eh?"

The Señora winced.

"Dinner will be at nine," she said, with the graciousness of a tigress to a visiting crocodile. "Everything in my poor house is at your disposal, señor." Her eyes warned him how seriously he would be permitted to take this as she rose in dismissal.

"My daughter," she said in passing, "could play a considerable part in your advertising schemes; like 'Miss Rheingold,' for example."

Mr Cobbleigh stayed in Portsbourne for a week, settling details of the merger. Meanwhile, in London, Denis was going regularly to Dr. Finlay. Step by careful step the doctor was taking his patient back, through school, through kindergarten, through early ecstasies and disappointments, towards that fatal plunge into the vat of stout.

Midweek, Denis was startled by a telegram from his uncle— Cobbleigh never wrote letters—saying:

"What the devil's Rhein-gold? Research, please."

Denis took out *The Ring of the Nibelung* from the library and dutifully ploughed through it. Woglinde, Wellgunde, and Flosshilde, the silvery Rhinemaidens, began to float and dart through his imagination along with the more sober and slow-moving octopi. Dr. Finlay took this development calmly.

"Don't discourage them," he said. "You have to get worse before you can get better. They may bring on a climax."

That night, as Denis lay on his sultry and haunted couch, his waking dream was cleft by a faraway call:

"Weia! Waga! Woge, du Welle, walle zur Wiege . . ."

An octopus, which had lately taken to sleeping curled up at his feet, skittered away, disturbed, and Denis, turning in wonderment, saw beside him a nixie, a sylph with a body as firm, green, and cool as an iced avocado, with upward-floating tresses which wavered as though adrift in an invisible current, with enchanting slanting eyes.

"Woglinde," she sang, laughing into his astonished face, "Woglinde and her sisters come to bid you share our frolic. Come! Look!"

She caught his fevered hand in her cool one and drew him to the edge of the bed. Below, in place of Axminster carpet, he saw illimitable depths of green and glimmering dark, shot with luminosity. Two more maidens, laughing and treading water, waited to welcome him.

Denis hesitated no longer. With a clean, curving dive he shot smoothly downwards into the waiting arms of Flosshilde and Wellgunde.

Mr Cobbleigh was in a baddish mood when he returned to London.

True, the takeover was complete, but the Señora Jerez was no mean businesswoman, and she had bested him on a number of minor points. By the end of the week he had had more than enough of her haughty Spanish ways. A crime to mix her aristocratic sherry with his plebeian stout, was it? He'd soon see about that!

When he found out that Denis had been going to a psychiatrist his annoyance was quadrupled. Denis had never seen him other than benevolent before, and was horrified. His uncle went small and evil with rage, like a venomous toad.

"How dare ye! How dare ye sneak off as soon's my back's turned?"

"But Uncle Dion, the sleeplessness was driving me mad!"

"And isn't that just the way I want ye? Isn't it in those waking nightmares of yours ye come up with hell's own wonderful notions for advertising campaigns? Let's have no more of it."

Denis, enchanted with the company of his new nightly playmates and determined at all costs not to lose them, had been almost ready to leave Dr. Finlay of his own accord, but this command put his back up; he continued his visits secretly.

———

Uncle Dion had another shock in store for him. "Ye're going to be married, my boy—don't scowl at me like that!—to the heiress of Avon Gold. The date of the wedding's set for November, so ye'd best go down and get to know the lovely Rosita. Also she's to be Miss Stout 1960, in a dress by Sacque of Longchamps, so there's work to be done, work to be done. Here's her photograph."

Denis was appalled. "You can't make me marry her!"

"Can't I just? What's wrong with her, anyway?"

"I can't endure that big black-eyed, sulky type." Small and fair, sang his mind, small and fair and green-limbed in the hither-and-thithering waters swim those I love.

"Nonsense! She's a grand handful."

"Anyway, you can't call the girl Miss Stout."

"Now, Denis, me broth of a boy," coaxed Uncle Dion, "ye mustn't throw a temperament on me at this delicate time. I'll strike a bargain with ye—a grand, wonderful advertising campaign from you to celebrate the takeover, and then ye can leave off the pills, take whatever treatment it is ye hanker for, and sleep all ye like. Make up for all the sleep ye've ever lost!"

"*Leave off the pills?* Are they what's been keeping me awake?"

Uncle Dion's eyes slid sideways. He was abashed. He had not meant to let loose that piece of information.

"Of all the heartless, sadistic—"

"Now, now, come, come, Denis, me boy. What's a little trick like that in the family? After all, don't forget what you owe me. I did pull you out of the vat of stout when you were four."

"I wish you'd left me to drown in it!" cried Denis with feeling.

The dry, brown summer crept towards its close. The campaign with Rosita as Miss Stout 1960 moved jerkily under way. Rosita flung herself into it enthusiastically. She was a girl with unbounded energy. The more Denis saw of her—and there was plenty to see—the more he disliked her.

She maintained an attitude both lofty and proprietorial towards him. He had hoped that she might be put off by his attendant octopi, but she seemed unable to see them.

"You won't mind the fact that I am completely unable to sleep?" he suggested.

"It gives us all the more time, doesn't it?" she countered, sending him a glance like a sizzling backhand.

Woglinde, Wellgunde, Flosshilde, come to my aid! Denis called inwardly, despairingly. But the Rhine sisters had retreated as Dr. Finlay's course of treatment inched onward towards its end; only sometimes at night an echo of their silvery laughter recalled his lost delights. Desperate, he turned to his uncle's pills again, but all they gave was a turbid series of images: porcupine, platypus, and armadillo.

He was due for his final session with the doctor on the afternoon before going down to Portsbourne for the official engagement party. Relaxed under hypnosis he had come at last to his fourth birthday, to the trip over the Liffey to his uncle's brewery, to the very lip of the vat of stout.

"I am standing with my mother, holding my sailor hat with its fluttering ribbons. Uncle Dion, who is as drunk as a trout, is dancing on the edge and singing the *Spanish Lady*. He slips and falls in. I jump in to rescue him; I have already learnt to swim in the Liffey, unknown to my mother. My hat falls in, too. Its wet ribbons get in my eyes and scare me for a moment; I think they are an octopus. I pull Uncle Dion to the side. I climb out . . ."

His voice faded away, lost in amazement. "*I rescued him!* He didn't pull me out! I pulled Uncle Dion out!"

With a shout of joy he kicked a small octopus under Dr. Finlay's desk and ran from the room.

Uncle Dion was in Portsbourne already. Denis caught the next train down. His heart was as light as the foam on a glass of pale ale. He was free! He was under no crushing obligation of gratitude! His uncle had been fooling him all these years. What matter a few residual octopi (one was sitting beside him on the seat)? He would soon get rid of them.

Now he could leave the business, he could write poetry instead of advertising doggerel, he could sleep all he wanted, and best of all he need not marry Rosita! He was free!

To prove his liberation from old fetters he went along to the restaurant car, ordered a sherry and a glass of Cobbleigh's Cream, mixed them under the fascinated eyes of the barman, and swigged them down.

"Everybody will be doing it soon," he said. "You may as well get used to it. Cobbleigh's Cobbler. It's a fine drink, too. Makes you won-der-ful-ly drowsy . . ."

By the time Denis left his taxi at El Hacienda he was sleepwalking. He glided like a cloud into the Señora's highly superior party, kissed her hand with a finished grace, and bowed to his uncle, who stood beside her like a wicked silver-haired gnome.

"I'm asleep," he announced. "I doubt if I shall ever wake again. I am not going to marry Rosita; instead I have made over to her my share in the firm. Good-bye, my dear uncle. I hope octopi haunt you till you die."

Before any of the startled guests could intercept him, he was out of the house again.

"Stop him!" shouted Uncle Dion furiously. "He's asleep! He'll do himself a mischief!"

They streamed out into the windy autumn night. A copper-coloured moon flung their shadows down the hillside. Far below, the little figure of Denis ran kicking its heels and laughing for joy.

"He'll go out on the bridge—he's going! Stop him!"

They raced after him, but his start was far too great. In the centre of the large sweep he turned, bowed again, and flung off his coat. He poised, and dived. A cold sigh of terrified anticipation went up from the watching guests. But nothing, no height, no fall, can hurt a sleep-walker. Down he soared like a falling leaf, and three pairs of green arms rose from the river to receive him.

Whether Denis ever woke again remained a matter for speculation, as he was never seen again.

Uncle Dion perished soon after from a surfeit of octopi; he saw them everywhere, in his bath, in his golf bag, even in his porridge.

The Señora and Rosita carried on the joint businesses success-fully for several years, until Rosita ran off and married a matador.

The Magnesia Tree

Like large plums fallen soggily to earth, the mayor and corporation of Ryme stood in the garden of Nathaniel Bond's house and looked at the Magnesia Tree.

The house itself was not remarkable—a long brown facade set back from the street across a cobbled courtyard; shuttered windows, a weathercock stuck perpetually at northeast. There were more beautiful sights in the town, which itself rose proudly out of the sea marshes, symmetrical as a volcano. But the mayor and aldermen felt, perhaps rightly, that there was a greater spiritual value in the house of a master of letters than in thirteenth-century tapestries or early fonts. Nathaniel Bond had been dead only a few weeks, and his house was to become a museum, left exactly as it had been when he was alive.

They were discussing it now.

Mr Bond had not been one of the ivory tower school. He had belonged to the *monde* and had entertained in his house celebrities and distinguished personages from all nations. In particular he numbered among his acquaintances many elegant elderly ladies who would arrive, stepping with a swish of skirt and ostrich plume from the London train into Mr Bond's brougham, in time for afternoon tea, that delectable meal, always taken, in summer, on the cobbled terrace underneath the Magnesia Tree.

There, by the hour, Mr Bond and his lady guest would gossip and chat—but what informed gossip, what scintillating chat—in full view, but out of earshot, of the passersby along Seagull Street, who thereby felt that they were being admitted to a view of one of the rites of literature.

Presently the lady would rise, bidding Nathaniel farewell, and be swept away, almost visibly, into the whirlpool of fashionable London society; into which Mr Bond himself took not infrequent plunges.

Here, though, was the corporation of Ryme and the mayor herself, Councillor Mrs Tunn, looking solemnly at the tree, standing in a ring round it as if, the august owner safely out of the way, they were meditating some game of elephantine Ring o' Roses. Their expressions were not playful, however; the tree was in fault; and they had been obliged to call in an expert at municipal expense to advise them on its condition. In fact their newly acquired property, which should have been a pure source of income and an attraction for tourists, was already proving a liability.

"Ever since Nathaniel Bond died," Councillor Sekville was explaining to the tree specialist from East Malling, "the tree has been failing."

The specialist, Professor Lombard, nodded judicially and walked round the tree. It was tall, with glossy star-shaped leaves, and flowers which should have been a brilliant orange but had faded to a not disagreeable salmon pink as a result of the tree's infirmity. Around the bole, which rose smoothly for some ten feet before branching, was built a rustic table and this made it impossible to approach the tree with any degree of familiarity. Professor Lombard leaned across the table and attempted to touch the bark.

"I shouldn't do that, sir, if I were you," said old Rust, the gardener, who had remained so far respectfully at the rear of the group.

"It won't bite, will it?" asked the professor rather frostily, but withdrawing his hand.

"Ah, its bark is worse than its bite, sir, if you'll pardon my witticism," replied Rust. "There's no knowing what that tree might do, now Mr Bond is no more."

The members of the corporation tittered somewhat derisively, but Professor Lombard took the gardener's statement seriously enough.

"There was an affinity between Mr Bond and the tree?"

"No, sir," answered Rust. "There was an antipathy. You could put it that Mr Bond hated the tree."

"In that case, why didn't he cut it down?"

"We knew well that if the tree were to die, it would be as good as tolling the knell for his own funeral."

"And conversely, if he died the tree would follow his example?"

"Who's to say, sir? One's dead, and one's dying, and it would take a wiser man than either of ourselves to know which began it. A tree takes longer to live than a man, and longer to die, too."

"Why did he hate the tree?"

"Ah, sir, now you're asking something which, properly speaking, falls outside my province."

The two men had fallen into step side by side and were walking up and down somewhat apart from the party of councillors, which by now had been augmented by a number of inquisitive sightseers and townspeople, attracted across the courtyard from Seagull Street.

"In my opinion that tree had a gift, or you might say a power," the gardener continued. "If you touched it, a feeling went tingling up your arm like the shock from an electric fence. And the aftermath of that shock made the mind wonderfully clear and calm. Many's the time, after I've pruned the tree or tended it in some way, that I've felt the inside of my head like a goldfish bowl—clean, transparent, the fish swimming round at ease with plenty of room; if I'd ever learned to write, I've often thought that would be the time when I'd write a piece of poetry."

"You can't write then?"

"No, sir, nor read either. That was why Mr Bond didn't mind my touching the tree. But touch it himself he never did, nor allow anyone else to do so."

"I should have expected a writer to be anxious for such an experience."

"Not Mr Bond, sir. Of course, I've never read any of his books but I understand that his line of writing was very different from the feeling I've mentioned. He was always one to have things complicated; he'd like a dahlia, if you follow me, sir, better than a primrose. That was why he disliked the tree, I suppose; many's the time I've seen him willfully teasing it, sitting beneath with one of his guests, chatting away, and the tree feeling left out and set at naught, I've no doubt at all; it would be enough to turn the nature sour in its veins."

"Do you think there is any hope for it?"

The gardener shook his head.

The onlookers by this time were becoming somewhat impatient, so Professor Lombard communicated to them the fruit of his conversation with Rust.

"What a monstrous man!" exclaimed the forthright Mrs Tunn. "He made no use of the tree himself and would not allow other writers to do so."

"He encouraged imitators, but never rivals," severely remarked the town librarian, Councillor Bull.

"Perhaps if the tree really is a source of inspiration to writers, we should advertise the fact and allow them to touch it for a small fee—say ten guineas," suggested Councillor Cockrich.

"There is the question as to whether it still possesses the same power," pointed out Professor Lombard. "Rust here seems to think that with the death of Nathaniel Bond, the tree's power may have altered in some way."

"But how are we to discover if that is so?"

"The only way would be to touch it."

The members of the assembly looked at each other and fell back a pace or two. No one seemed anxious to make the attempt. The professor asked Rust if he would care to, but the old gardener shook his head.

"I'm a married man, sir. If that tree's diseased or gone astray in some way there's still power enough there to do a plenty harm, I'm sure of that."

"Supposing we leave the matter for a few days and refer it to committee," suggested Mrs Tunn. "Professor Lombard has done all he can for us. We must put a policeman on duty to make sure that no unauthorised person touches the tree in the meantime."

The other officials felt that this was a very proper solution to a problem which was inconveniently out of their scope, involving, as it did, moral and literary questions of which they neither took, nor wished to take, cognisance. They departed with dignity.

By this time, however their number had been far outweighed by the group of leisured citizens who had strolled into the courtyard and who remained, chatting among themselves and gazing speculatively at the tree.

A reserved-looking young man on the outermost fringe of this crowd appeared to have taken a particularly keen interest in the discussion, and he now made his way up to the tree as if he intended to touch it. He was, however, warned off by the policeman who had been summoned, and he retreated to his former position, much abashed. His name was Mr Smith, and he was a smallholder, very small indeed, who lived just beyond the town wall and had the presumption to try and illuminate his somewhat miserable existence by writing poetry.

In the past he had often been struck with awe by the fact that the town of which he was a citizen also contained such a notable literary figure as Nathaniel Bond. Only once had he actually met the writer, in the bookshop, and he had then timidly inquired:

"Are you not, sir, Nathaniel Bond?"

"Yes, I am," snapped Mr Bond, turning on him waspishly, "and what is that to you?"

"Nothing, nothing," replied the young man in terror, and he retreated at once into the street. He had been shocked at his own pre-sumption and never again ventured to try and strike up acquaintance with the great. Gazing around the courtyard now he was surprised to see how many well-known literary and social personalities were among his fellow citizens. He led such an extremely self-contained life among his cows and poultry that for months on end he tended to forget that there were other human beings living in the town at all.

"But you see, Colin," cried an elegant lady with a hawklike pro-file, clad entirely in grey except for the sparkle of diamonds at her wrist, "but you see I am his executrix, and it is my most painful duty to stay here until the council—poor blindworms that they are—have decided on the arrangements for the Nathaniel Bond museum."

"My poor Cecilia," said the man she addressed, who must, Mr Smith thought, be the poet Colin Warlock, "how devastating for you. Do not on any account let feminine curiosity tempt you into touching the tree. It would be just like one of dear Nat's malicious little jokes if it at once turned you into a Salvation Lassie."

The Honourable Cecilia Fontriver gave a little shriek of dismay.

The townspeople slowly dispersed until there was nobody left but the policeman, stolidly mounting guard by the tree, the young man wistfully staring at it, and the Hon. Cecilia, who had sunk languidly into a wicker chair and was fanning herself.

"Do you think that the tree would turn me into a Salvation Lassie?" she startled the young man by suddenly inquiring of him.

"I—really, madam, I can hardly venture to form an opinion, but it seems unlikely that if the power of the tree derives from Mr Bond, it would evince itself in such an unkind and unjust manner."

"Oh? And why do you think that Mr Bond would not be unjust or unkind, pray?" She eyed him coolly.

"Because he was great," he replied.

"Really? Do you think that the two things are incompatible? You are a very odd young man," she pursued, considering him through her lorgnette.

"I am a poet, madam."

"You are quite unlike the poets I am acquainted with."

"I am a very indifferent poet, I fear," he said modestly. "I feel that if only I had an opportunity of touching the tree, there would be a great improvement in my work."

"You are not afraid to touch it?"

"Oh no," he exclaimed ardently.

Mrs Fontriver considered him further. He was a very personable young man, she considered; more than "taking," positively "fetching."

"Come back here at eleven o'clock tonight," she commanded, laying a hand soft as velvet on his arm. "I will contrive that the police-man is elsewhere."

With a nod, she was gone indoors, who knows whether to muse over the Bondiana there displayed or to scan, with how objective an eye, her wardrobe in quest of a costume suitable for an upcoming occasion of such importance to literary science?

At eleven o'clock Mr Smith returned. Mrs Fontriver was already flitting in the shadows of the courtyard. She took his hand and led him in the direction of the tree. Then she paused, as if a thought had suddenly struck her.

"Should you perhaps come in first and sustain yourself with something from Nathaniel's cellar or a glance at his prints? It is surely ill-advised to undergo such an experience without some preparation?"

The glance from her dark eyes would have melted a gold candle-stick, but Mr Smith had thoughts only for the tree. He leaned to touch it and fell with a little cry across the rustic table, his face against the bark and his arms encircling the massive trunk.

Touching him, Mrs Fontriver discovered that he was dead. She looked at him crossly, shrugged her shoulders, and went in to bed.

Next day the tree, too, was dead—black and shriveled. It was hurriedly cut down and removed, together with the body of Mr Smith. He had been such an obscure young man that there was none to mourn him except, indeed, his Alderneys crowding distressfully round the cowshed door. But Mrs Fontriver, returning to London in her first-class carriage, thought of him with a touch of regret. He had, after all, been a very "fetching" young man.

Honeymaroon

A wave swung high and lazily, with a curve like the white breast of a pouter pigeon, swept little Miss Roe clean off the deck of the elderly immigrant ship where she lay sleeping in the sun, and sucked her back underwater without any noise or commotion; she vanished among sea-thistles, tangled ocean-daisies, foamtips crossing this way and that, and the glitter of fins bright as mica. Nobody noticed; she was just a typist, with no relations, on her way to look for a job.

She called for help in her tiny breathless voice and tried to swim, but the waves tired her out with their salty slaps on face and arms; presently she was unconscious, floating and drifting in the teeth of a wandering current that edged her through reefs and slid her up the beach of an island, itself little more than a spit of sand in the enormous shining sea.

After a time Miss Roe recovered consciousness. All she knew at first was the gritty shifting feel of sand that has had water over it a short time before, warm under her body. Then she raised herself on her forearms and looked about; she saw the gentle slope of the island to her left, and the smooth sea, with a curdle of reefs far out, on her right. She brushed off the damp sand and sat up.

There was a salt taste on her lips, not unlike anchovies, not unpleasant; she licked them once or twice and tried to smooth the knots out of her sticky hair before starting off to look for help. She was still wearing her faded old sunsuit, so she was decent enough.

Barefooted she paddled over the hot, yielding sand and found to her dismay that the island was small, circular, and uninhabited. It consisted of nothing but sandhills, save that in the centre there were two springs, one hot, one cold.

The hot spring bubbled and seethed in its own ferment of boiling mud, sinking away as fast as it rose. The cold spring, hardly bigger, nourished a couple of date palms whose long silky leaves, whispering above, cast a small patch of shade into which Miss Roe gratefully dropped.

Clusters of dates hung from the branches: she would not lack food. She ate a few absently, though she was not hungry. Rested, she began again her weary, useless pacing of this simplified horizon. Near the tops of the sandhills she saw small holes, but she prudently avoided them. She had been told that large spiders sometimes live in sand.

Two days passed. Miss Roe was not precisely unhappy, since she had no friends to pine for, but she was lonely, and desperately in need of occupation. Never much of a one to read, she was accustomed always to have in hand some piece of knitting or crochet, outside of office hours, and the unwonted lack of exercise for her supple fingers irked her terribly. There was no material on the island at all; only the sand and the palm trees, whose leaves were too brittle and sharp for satisfactory use.

On the afternoon of the second day, Miss Roe was lying by the cool spring, idly watching the water well up and then seep back into the damp sand. Already she was tanned by the sun; her slight body had taken the same colour as the sand she lay on, and her unimpressive mouse-coloured hair was bleaching to a silvery floss.

She saw two little brown things like bits of fluff approaching. For one heart-sickening moment she thought that they were spiders, and then, on a breath of relief, perceived that they were in fact mice; small golden-brown mice with bright needlepoint eyes and long, extra-long tails, each ending in a tidy tassel like a miniature feather duster. Normally she was afraid of mice, but these seemed unconnected with the dirty, furtive scufflings behind cheese crock or bread bin which were all her previous experience. They approached with caution, true, but with dignity, pausing at her slightest movement, putting their heads together as if they conferred, and then nimbling on again.

When they were only a couple of feet from her they stopped and went into a great pantomime, nodding their heads, flashing their almost invisible whiskers, gesturing with tiny hands and above all with their elongated mobile tails which whipped to and fro over their backs.

Miss Roe was not at all intelligent, but even she could see that they were communicating with each other, and attempting to do so with her.

It took them six months to teach her their language.

The mice lived in tiny cavelike hollows in the sand, shored and lined everywhere inside with slender sea twigs that were polished white as ivory by the passing of countless furry bodies. Their principal food was dried fish-flakes, savoury, of a soft leaflike consistency, and silver-brown in colour. While she was lying unconscious the mice had fed Miss Roe with these; they were highly nutritious and contained vitamin D in large quantities.

It was some time before the mice, whose intelligence was of a high order, realised that Miss Roe was almost totally ignorant about the workings of the civilisation from which she had come. At first they questioned her severely on ethics, civics, mathematics, and other topics, but in the end they resigned themselves to the fact that her mind contained little beyond an exhaustive knowledge of knitting patterns and the difference between right and wrong.

They did, however, become very fond of Miss Roe, and when they saw her pining for lack of occupation they started a fur collection, bringing her little heaps of moulted mousedown which her skilful fingers twirled into threads and knitted on palm-frond needles into various unnecessary articles.

When rescue appeared, in the form of a shabby schooner anchored outside the reef, the mice were saddened by the prospect of Miss Roe's departure.

Tears stood in her guileless eyes also.

"Isn't there anything I can do for you?" she begged. "You've been so kind to me! I could ask them to leave some cheese—or—or books so that you could learn to read—?"

Tass, the senior mouse, looked at her very kindly. His whiskers were grey, his eyes were twinkling. In appearance he was not unlike Einstein.

"The greatest service you can do us," he said, "is to tell no one of our existence. Can you promise that?"

"Of *course* I can!" She scrubbed the shine from her eyes with the back of a brown hand. "Is there truly nothing else?"

"Yes," he said dryly, "you can take those two young hotheads, Afi and Anep, with you, and rid our happy republic of a pair of troublemakers."

Afi and Anep joyfully accepted the chance to travel. And so, when the crew of the dinghy neared the shore, there was nothing to see but a solitary figure on a bare and uninhabited island. With astonishment they saw Miss Roe, slender and brown, wearing—for this was during the cool equinoctial winds—a bikini and thick sweater of mousewool which many an Italian starlet might have envied. They did not see Afi and Anep, the two young demagogues, whose bright little beady black eyes peered glancingly out through the cable-stitch from their snug hiding place inside her big roll collar.

"Cripes," said Ant Arson, "wait till the captain sees this."

"You'd better wait," muttered Singer Jones, "or Cap'll feed you to the tiburones." And he shunted his jaw sideways with a meaning leer.

The boat's crew seemed haloed with gold to Miss Roe as they pulled towards her. Actually they were as unsavoury a load as might have been found anywhere in the South Pacific, and their captain was a fit leader for them.

Valentino MacTavish mooched about the ocean with his unshaven crew and his shocking old ship full of unmentionable cargoes, carrying on a dozen illegal trades, engaging in acts of minor piracy when it seemed safe, wanted by the police of every large port but always slipping away just before the net descended.

"Man!" said Valentino MacTavish, eyeing Miss Roe with the incredulity of a cat that sees a whole Dover sole laid on its dish. And he helped her over the gunwale.

She noticed first that the *Aurora* seemed full of dirty washing and sardine tins; second, that the captain, though very attentive in a queer way, was not much like Alec Guinness, her ideal of seamanly beauty; third, that the crew, huddled together in the waist, seemed jeeringly in awe of their captain; fourth, that the two totalitarian mice in her collar were becoming restive, possibly because their sharp nostrils detected the odour of proletarian comrades somewhere near at hand.

"I should like to wash my hands, please," she said, and was taken with suspicious promptitude to Valentino's cabin.

The mess and clutter depressed her. She found herself regretting the tidy island and friendly mice, feeling homesick.

She shook Afi and Anep out of her collar, and they rushed greedily about the floor, questing and roving among the discarded underwear and heady unfamiliar smells, presently making off down holes in the panelling to preach equality and the rights of mice. From time to time they darted joyously back to report on their successes with the ship's rodent population.

"Do be careful!" Miss Roe exclaimed anxiously. "The captain said he was coming back soon to show me round."

"We won't let him see us."

They waved their tails in reassurance.

As it happened, they were both sitting on her shoulders, Anep telling her how he had set up committees to form trade unions, Afi reporting a lecture he had delivered to the boiler-room mice on the need for collective ownership of the means of production—when the door opened and Captain MacTavish came in. There was just time to fly under her collar once more.

Valentino carried a bottle of palm wine under his arm. He had already drunk half of it. Now he took another swig, put down the bottle, and advanced on Miss Roe in a purposeful manner.

His mind was fuddled with drink, a suspicion that his crew were laughing at him, and the need for asserting his authority. A core of anger, mainly at himself, burnt in him; his eyes were bloodshot, shamed, and lustful. In many ways he was a piteous object.

To his astonishment, when he laid hold of the petrified Miss Roe, his amatory intentions were interrupted by a series of savage, needlesharp stabs in his left wrist and right forearm.

He shrieked, clawing at his arms, and shrieked again as, like animated scalpels, the two mice dived for his most vulnerable points.

The crew heard shrieks coming from the cabin, but this was a commonplace. True, the voice sounded like the captain's rather than the girl's, but Valentino was an eccentric, and it would have been the height of indelicacy to intrude—and, anyway, more than their lives were worth.

They settled down on the after-hatch, throwing numbered sardine tins for the chance of being next with the girl.

A couple of hours later someone gave a shout, and the crew, focusing their eyes as best they could, saw a raft drifting in the *Aurora*'s direction.

"Hey, fellas, there's someone on it."

"It's the crazy Swede. You know? Olaf Myrdal."

"Think we oughta tell Cap?"

"Better not."

"Ah, shucks, we can disturb him by now, surely?"

Ant went down and peered through the cabin keyhole. The yell he let out brought the rest of the crew running, and in panicked incredulity they broke open the door.

Miss Roe was lying on the floor, deeply unconscious. At some distance from her lay a skeleton, white and shining.

It was not until Singer touched the bones and discovered them to be warm that real terror set in.

"Where in heck's it come from?" bellowed Ant, frightened and sweating, looking for reassurance to the others.

"Where's Cap?"

"But look—look," stuttered Dice Morgan. "Look at that finger!"

They looked. On a metacarpal bone shone a band of tarnished gold with a familiar amethyst. The captain had been something of a dandy.

"Good sakes!" breathed Ant. "It's *him!* It *is* Cap!" Fear soon finds relief in vengeance.

"The girl's done it! Drop her over the side! Feed her to the sharks. She's a witch, she's a Jonah."

Several of the crew were averse to touching Miss Roe at all, but Singer was not so particular, and he dragged her unconscious body on deck.

"Why not put her on the raft?" suggested Dice brilliantly. "We don't want her haunting us. We drop her overboard, the sharks eat her, we get her duppy climbing up the side every night and pulling us in by the ankles. Put her on the raft, let her haunt the loony Swede."

There was a chorus of agreement.

They hailed the raft, which was now floating past their stern.

"Hi there, you Swede! Will you take a bit of cargo for us?"

The Swede came to the door of his little cabin and surveyed them coldly.

"I wish for nothing that has been on your ship," he said. But already two men had grappled the raft alongside, and two more wrapped Miss Roe's body in a tarpaulin and rolled it over the gunwale. More by luck than judgment it fell on the balsawood deck of the raft.

"Adios, amigos!" shouted the crew of *Aurora*, leaning over the stern-rail and waving. "Have a happy honeymoon! Mind she don't turn you to a skellington, Swedey! Disconnecta dem dry bones!"

They drew away. The Swede reluctantly removed the wrappings from the bundle they had tossed him. When he saw Miss Roe, his expression of disapproval deepened. He scooped up a dipper of seawater and dashed it in her face.

Presently she came to, looked round her, and shuddered.

"Did they hurt you?" he said.

Her eyes slowly took him in—his bigness, his slow, gentle movements, his look of rather severe intelligence.

"Who are you? You don't look like those men." She pulled herself to a sitting position. "Am I still on the ship?"

"You are not on the ship, no. They threw you off. Have they injured you?"

Her eyes dilated. "He was going to—that captain! But the mice—it was horrible!" Suddenly she stiffened. "The mice! Afi and Anep—where are they?"

Afi ran from her collar and rubbed affectionately against her chin. She stroked him in relief. The Swede's expression softened as he observed this exchange. But then Miss Roe burst into tears.

"Do not cry, young lady. I do not know what you were doing on that ship, and I may say frankly that I did not wish for a passenger, especially a female one, but I think you are better off here than there. Wait, and I will make some seaweed tea. My name is Olaf Myrdal," he added with a certain dignity. "You may have heard of me."

"It's my mouse," sobbed poor Miss Roe, unheeding. "The other mouse, Anep! He's been left on that ship. Oh please, please go back and fetch him."

"Impossible, my dear child," he said gently. "That ship has a far greater command of speed than my raft, and, as you can see, it is nearly five miles ahead of us."

Since Miss Roe continued to weep unrestrainedly, he said after a while, with a slightly admonishing air, "I think you had better tell me all about it."

Miss Roe calmed down as she told her story. She couldn't help liking and trusting this tall, quiet man with his long sweeping golden beard and his benign expression.

The expression changed to one of qualified surprise as her story proceeded.

"So!" he said. "An island of intelligent mice. I should indeed like to call there. And you can communicate with them?"

"Yes," said Miss Roe, wiping her eyes, "we used to have ever such nice talks in the evenings. You'd be surprised what a lot goes through their little heads."

"This mouse you have here is one of them?"

Afi was prospecting busily about the raft, sniffing, tasting, and scrutinising.

"Can you request your small friend to come here?"

Miss Roe called Afi, who ran confidingly up her leg and from the eminence of her wrist looked in a searching manner at Myrdal.

"Does this man come from your country?" he asked Miss Roe. She shook her head. "Excellent," the mouse remarked, "then perhaps he can tell me things you do not know. Ask if in his land they have nationalised the means of production?"

Miss Roe translated this as best she could. Myrdal's eyebrows shot up.

"Doesn't he know?" said Afi, disappointed. "Well, ask him if he is familiar with these concepts: the transition of quantity into quality, the negation of the negation, the interpenetration of opposites?"

"Merciful heavens!" exclaimed the Swede. "To think that I, who have come to sea in order to escape once and for all from mankind's violence and the conflicts of warring ideologies, should have run up against a Marxist mouse."

Miss Roe, accustomed to the philosophical talk of her mouse friends, was still unhappy.

"What about poor Anep," she mourned, "alone on that ship, among those dreadful men?"

"He will be in no danger. If, as you tell me, he has already organised the ship's mice into trade unions, it is for the men that you should fear. Already they are doomed. Already, maybe, they have suffered the fate of their captain. And when the ship reaches port, what then? I believe that you have loosed on mankind, unwittingly, a greater destructive force than the hydrogen bomb. The age of men is ended; that of mice is about to begin."

"Oh dear," said Miss Roe. "Do you think we might have some of that seaweed tea you talked about?" It always took her a little while to assimilate an idea.

"When do *we* reach port?" she asked later, sipping the hot green fluid.

"Never."

"Never? But—"

"Did I not tell you that I came to sea to escape from violence? More than ever now it will be necessary to stay away from the world of men. I have ample resources on the raft—the works of Strindberg, Ibsen, Thomas Hardy, Voltaire, and Shakespeare."

Miss Roe seemed doubtful of these benefits. Then she brightened. "Couldn't we go back to my island?"

"My dear girl, there is nothing I should like better, in due course. But for the moment it would be out of the question. Afi is now a potential menace to the island's peace, since he has had experience of the efficacy of violence. Also—though this is merely a personal consideration—our own lives might be in danger if he were able to tell the other mice about the experiment with Captain MacTavish. They might wish to repeat it—especially as you promised not to reveal their existence and have done so."

"Yes—I see." But Miss Roe could hardly believe it of her dear mice.

"Mice do not live long," pronounced Olaf. "We can afford to drift for a year or two, until Afi dies of old age, before we return."

"Poor Afi ! He will be rather bored. He was hoping to get to Australia."

"I shall learn his language and teach him Swedish; we shall have philosophical discussions. I shall read him Strindberg, also."

"I suppose you haven't any wool or knitting needles, have you?" said Miss Roe wistfully, feeling a little left out by this programme. He shook his head.

"Another thing," he said. "We must be married. For a young girl and a man, even a philosopher like me, to drift about the ocean on a raft without matrimony is not at all seemly."

Married! Miss Roe stared in surprise that approached conster-nation at this godlike being who spoke the word so matter-of-factly. Never, never, in her wildest dreams . . .

"But how could we?" she said. "There's no church, no clergyman?"

"Marriage before witnesses is quite correct at sea. Your friend down there is rational—he will do admirably as a witness."

Miss Roe's eyes began to shine. This put a different complex-ion on things. If she were married to this Mr Myrdal, he would not seem quite so alarming; and she could endure the solemnity of drift-ing about the Pacific reading Strindberg aloud to a mouse if she was graced with the status of a married woman.

"But mind," he said, "no children!"

"No children?" She was dreadfully cast down. "But if all the world is going to be overrun with mice, surely it's our duty—?"

"My belief is that the human race is due to expire. It shall not be our part to prolong its death-throes."

"Oh dear," said Miss Roe again.

The simple marriage ceremony was performed. Afterwards Olaf and Afi, who had taken a great fancy to one another, settled down to a discussion of the philosophy of Kant.

Miss Roe, now Mrs Myrdal, stretched out in the rays of the setting sun, chin propped on elbows, and watched them. He was nice, her new husband, she decided: a bit silly with all his fanciful ideas perhaps, a bit grand and dignified, but ever so kind! And all men had to be learnt and managed. It was a shame about the children, though; she had already planned to ask if she couldn't snip off a bit of that long, golden beard. It would knit up lovely into tiny bootees.

Oh well—she stretched, and rolled over into the last of the sunshine—there would be plenty of time to persuade him to change his mind.

Harp Music

It wasn't till long afterwards that Father told me about his journey home with the harp. At the time it had gone too deep.

It all began one morning when I was cleaning the windows of the bus we lived in. There were a lot of windows, and they took a lot of cleaning, but when you'd done justice to them and the sun came out the effect was fine.

Father was asleep after night-shift, in the big double folding bed, and Coffee the cat was stretched out at full stretch on top of him. They were both very large, and they had found that was more satisfactory than trying to partition the bed between them.

I'd finished the main windows and was in the cab, which we'd converted to other uses by taking out the driving seat. I was just giving the windscreen a final polish when I heard bumping and realised with astonishment that Father was getting up of his own accord—getting up without my beseeching and begging and bullying him to do so, without even a cup of tea. There was a clink as he put the teapot on the stove to boil up, and I went in to see what was going on.

"It's not time for you to wake yet," I said. "Only half past eleven."

"I'm going out to buy a harp," Father said, pulling his belt through the slots that he always cut in the tops of his trousers.

He was amazingly cheerful. Normally he hated the whole process of washing and dressing; he'd get through it as fast as possible in a glum silence. But this morning he burst into song, a song about virgin sturgeon of which the less quoted the better. When I came back from emptying my bucket, I was thunderstruck to see that Father had on his old A.R.P. warden's coat and was gulping a hasty pint of boiling, rust-coloured tea before leaving.

"Don't you want any breakfast?" I said.

"No," he said. He didn't eat much breakfast at the best of times, and never before he'd been up and smoking for an hour.

He went outside and took the tarpaulin off his bicycle. "See you at midnight."

"Won't you be back before?" I said.

"I told you, I'm going to buy a harp." He started off across the field. Midway, a thought struck him. He turned and summoned me with wavings of his arms. I trotted across.

"Oh, by the way," he said, "there's a girl coming to leave some things."

"A girl?"

"Yes," he said impatiently. "A girl from the office." Father was a rewrite man at a news agency. "She's divorcing her husband. They can't agree about which of their belongings are his and which are hers, so she wants to leave a couple of her treasures with me for safekeeping in case he tries to grab them and hide them away. I said she could."

"What are the things?"

"Heaven knows. A clock, maybe, or a typewriter."

"We haven't much space," I said, looking doubtfully back at the bus. It was only a single-decker.

"It won't be for more than a month or two. Till the divorce is through," Father said optimistically. He got on his bike again.

"What's her name?" I called.

"Can't remember. Beryl something. What are those bread things you put in soup?" he called back.

"Croutons?"

"That's it. Well—be seeing you." This time he really was off.

I went back to the bus feeling rather forlorn, resenting this Mrs Crouton, and folded up the bed with a heave and a clang. Then I had to unfold it again because Coffee the cat was still inside.

At about half past two I heard a tap on the window and sticking my head out I saw a pretty but distracted-looking redhead. She was rather shabbily dressed, but the tiny man beside her might just that minute have stepped out of a polythene bag. Beyond the field gate stood an enormous car. A queer thread of sound which I couldn't identify seemed to be coming from the front of the bus. I went outside and the noise identified itself; a baby in a pram was parked by the bonnet.

"Are you Mrs Crouton?" I said. A horrible feeling of uneasiness was beginning to grow in me.

"Crouton?" she said, seeming surprised. "No, I'm Beryl Sippett. Are you Sean Ross?"

"Yes."

"Oh, good. Your father said I could leave my baby here."

"Baby?"

"Yes, and the dog. Here, Tweetie, Tweetie!" A skeletal poodle raced out from under the bus.

"He didn't say anything about a baby to me. He thought it was a clock."

"It's not for long," she said reassuringly. "Just for a few days till I find somewhere to live. I'm staying with my lawyer at the moment—this is my lawyer, Mr Glibchick—and he's only got a service flat, no place for a baby."

"But I don't know if I'll be able to look after it," I said more and more doubtfully. "And what about the dog?"

"Oh, they'll both be as good as gold, no trouble, I promise. I'm sure you can manage. Your father said you were an awfully reliable boy, and you look it, I must say."

"Come along, my dear," said the tiny Mr Glibchick, looking at his gold watch. "We shall be late for the magistrate's court, and it's most important to make a good impression." I didn't see how Mr Glibchick could fail to make a good impression; he was so smooth and prosperous-looking in his fur coat.

"Oh dear," said Beryl, suddenly crying a little. "I do hate to part with them really."

"Now, now, my dear, you're doing the best thing you possibly can do for them. That husband of yours is a brute, regular rotter, come now, isn't he? Much better where he can't find them." Mr Glibchick's delivery was very clear and rapid; he talked like someone trained on tongue-twisters.

They began to walk away. There were so many questions to ask that they jammed in my mind.

"What do they eat?" I yelped.

"Meat for Tweetie; and the baby eats absolutely everything— rhubarb, custard, mashed potato, cereal, egg—you know."

The huge grey car drifted away, silent as an elephant in the jungle. I was left alone, full of forebodings, with my two charges. Just let Father get home, I thought, and I'd have a word or two to say to him. Unfortunately he wouldn't be home till after midnight.

The main inconvenience about Father was his habit of helping people in difficulties. He'd do anything for them; nothing was too much trouble. He had an extraordinarily kind heart. The year before, he had discovered that one of the Americans in his office was home-sick. He spent two days catching a cricket in the dry stone wall at the side of our field, and another two days standing over me while I made a cage for it to live in, so that the homesick American should have a noise to remind him of Tennessee. That's the sort of person father was.

I will draw a veil over the rest of my day. Anyone who has looked after babies knows how they behave when they don't care for their surroundings. Anyone who hasn't looked after babies is in a state of enviable ignorance, and I will leave them that way. I will only mention that, after a good deal of experiment, I found one infallible method of stopping the baby's howls. This was to put it in the pram and race it at top speed (I should say here that I had won the fifteen years and under three-quarter mile at the village sports) round and round the field. The baby liked this. Unfortunately Tweetie the dog didn't care for it; he was nervous about my running, maybe he thought I was trying to kidnap the child, and insisted on racing beside me, taking a nip out of my calf every so often and barking in a high-pitched hysterical manner.

The evening wore on. At about half-past eleven the baby suddenly fell into an exhausted slumber. I could have gone to sleep, too, but I was hungry, having had nothing to eat since lunch. I cooked bacon, and gave some to Tweetie. He wouldn't touch it, but began to whine and snuffle despairingly. I think he was not a very intelligent dog and it had only just come home to him that his mistress had abandoned him in this uncongenial place.

Around this time, too, I realised that the low continuous noise from above, which I had taken for thunder, was actually Coffee the cat, who had retired to the luggage rack that ran below the roof of the bus and was making it plain that he didn't care for our guests.

I had lulled the baby to sleep in the pram outside, where it was easier to joggle. Now I decided reluctantly that as a heavy mist was coming up I'd better bring it in. I parked it in its carrycot in the driver's cab. It woke up and started to yell again.

Of course if I'd had Dr Spock's book in the bus I'd have known that it was probably suffering from three-month colic. And if we'd been on the telephone I could have rung up the Mansion House number that gives soothing advice to would-be suicides. As things were I just stood stock-still, in a sort of stupor of fatigue, wondering what to do next.

My gaze fell idly on the newspaper cutting stuck into the clock-face. It said, "Harp for sale, cheap," and gave an address in Essex. For the first time in nine hours I remembered that father had gone off to buy a harp. A harp, I thought, what does he want a harp for? And then the yells from the cab redoubled and I decided savagely that I wished he were getting a pair of wings and a halo, too, while he was at it.

I went and fished the baby out of its cot again, and walked up and down with it. Tweetie followed and sometimes bit me. Coffee growled overhead. Presently there was a loud bang at the door, and Tweetie burst into a fusillade of tremulous barks.

Meanwhile, Father had gone up to London and caught a train from Liverpool Street into the depths of Essex, finished his journey by taxi, and bought the harp. He said afterwards that it was cheap, but he wouldn't tell me how much. Anyway I don't know how much a harp ought to cost.

Father was always very much swayed by impulse, and since Mother died the impulses had been more and more impulsive. He couldn't just live along in an easy, day-to-day manner like everybody else, he needed a goal to aim at, or else something to fight. Just now the harp was his goal. Ever since he'd first seen the advertisement he couldn't rest or eat or breathe or sleep easy till he had it. His father—my grandfather—had had a mandolin on which he could play any tune by ear. Grandfather had perfect pitch, too, and could sing a natural tenor part, so I suppose it was reasonable that Father should suddenly want a harp. He had a very fine voice, too, and when mother was alive she used to play the piano for hours on end and Father used to sing.

He had to rush straight back from Essex to his office, taking the harp with him. It aroused a lot of interest among the men on the desk, but there was no time to play it; a Latin American president had been shot in a revolution and the wires were fairly humming. Father only just managed to get away for his train, and he had to gallop from end to end of Waterloo station, carrying the harp on his shoulder; a porter driving one of those long baggage-trains happened to cut across his line of progress, suddenly saw him, gasped, and muttered, "Blimey, it must be one of the perishers I run over come back to haunt me."

Father jumped over the link-rod and just caught his train.

All this time he had been borne up by the superhuman, manic strength and endurance which carried him along on such occasions. Ordinarily I doubt if he could lift a harp, but when he was in that state he could perform in a couple of hours feats that would take five men a week in normal conditions. By the finish he'd be chipped, scarred, panting, bleeding, and at the end of his resources, and would probably sleep for two days.

When he got out at our station he didn't try to ride his bike with the harp, however; he knew his limits. He started out to walk the last mile with the harp on his shoulder. Of course at that time of night the road was dark and quite deserted as a rule, but about halfway along father fell in with a man wheeling a pram.

"Nasty night," said father. It had begun to rain, and he was hurrying, anxious to get his precious harp under cover.

"Very," said the man. "Can you tell me if I'm going the right way to the station?"

"No, brother," said Father. "It's just the other way. But if you want a train, you'll be unlucky; the last one's just gone."

"Oh, Hades," said the man with feeling. "Now what am I going to do?" A faint squawk came from the pram.

"When's the first train in the morning?"

"Do you want somewhere to stay the night?" said Father at once. "Is that a baby in there? Can't let it spend the night on the station. I'll tell you what—you come back with me, I can put you up. You can share a bed with me. My boy won't mind sleeping on the floor; often done it."

"Well—" said the man, "that's very decent of you. If you're sure you don't mind?"

"Glad to," said Father enthusiastically. "Specially if I can dump my harp on your pram for the rest of the way."

"I suppose you play in an orchestra," said the man. He went on rather awkwardly, "I should explain that I don't usually tramp round with my baby in the small hours, but my fool of a wife's suddenly decided she wants a divorce, wants to marry her old wing-commander, and so she runs off with the nipper and for reasons best known to herself leaves it down here with some crazy journalist who lives in a bus. I only got the address by blasting it out of the secretary of her lawyer, who's a crook if ever there was one."

They came to the gate of the field.

"I live just through here," said Father . . .

Next morning we slept late. We were all dog-tired. There had been a good many explanations the night before. At first Mr Sippett wanted to take his pram and get right away from there; he thought we were a nest of kidnappers. But it was raining hard by then and the bus was very snug and cosy; moreover, luckily, he had taken a liking to Father, who always inspired instant trust and affection in people— unless they hated him on sight.

Father wanted to try the new harp, late though it was, but I put a stop to that; if the baby woke again, I said, I wasn't going to be the one to race round the field with it in the rain and dark. I shall never forget the wonderful relief it was when Mr Sippett knocked on the door and claimed his offspring. I have never been so glad to part with anything. It was a shock to see them coming back again with Father.

So we were all in a coma still next day, the two fathers on the bed with Coffee, the baby with me in the end room on layers and layers of *Times*es, and Tweetie on the doormat, when Beryl Sippett returned.

"Charles!" she exclaimed in amazement.

He stuck a bleary head out of the bedclothes and slowly took in the situation.

"Beryl," he said. He looked rather pleased to see her.

Then he became all of a sudden very angry.

"Do you know what you did?"

"No," she said, "what?"

"Went off, leaving the kitchen fire switched on and *the fridge door open!* Of all the feckless, extravagant—"

"Oh darling," she said, "did I? How awful. I am sorry."

Father had tried to pretend to himself while this was going on that he was not awake, but it was no use, so now he got out of bed and stumped past Mrs Sippett to the kitchen, giving her a gloomy nod on the way. He proceeded to shave while I made breakfast. Mercifully the baby was still asleep; I daresay it had some overtime to make up for.

During breakfast it was plain that the Sippetts had reconciled their matrimonial difficulties. Something had made Beryl lose faith in Mr Glibchick, or she had thought better of the wing-commander. They were both extremely warm in their thanks to us.

"I do love your bus," Mrs Sippett said, looking sentimentally round it, "and what a lovely view with the field and the pond. Really you and your little boy are lucky to live here."

"Yes, I suppose so," said Father in a glum voice. "Used to have a house when my wife was alive. Too much trouble now."

He looked moodily down at his slippers, which my frivolous mother had made him shortly before she died, out of coconut matting because she said it was the only material that would stand the wear. They had stood it pretty well for seven years.

After breakfast the Sippetts went off, arm in arm, with their pram and their dog, happily down the road to the station. At last Father could get to his harp. But somehow the fire had gone out of his desire to play it. He took the bicycle tarpaulin off it, surveyed it with a morose eye, and struck a couple of experimental chords. They sounded terrible. He tried another. It was worse.

"Bloody hell," my father said.

He looked once more, bitterly, after the silly, happy family of Sippetts, then picked up his harp with a last access of strength, carried it across the field, and hurled it into the pond.

The Sale of Midsummer

The van, which was labeled Modway Television, chugged up a long, steep hill, slipped thankfully into top gear, and ran down through fringes of beechwood bordering a small star-shaped valley which lay sunk in the top of the downs. Presently the trees ended and sunny curves of cowslip-studded grass began; ahead, clustered elms half revealed a few grey stone roofs.

"This ought to be it," Andrew said, looking at his map. "There's a village green; that'd be the best place to leave the van. I'll take the mike and you bring the camera, Tod, and we'll wander."

"What shall I do?" asked Bill, the van driver.

"Find the pub and get their recipe for cowslip wine. It's a speciality of the place."

"That'll suit me fine."

Among the elms grouped in pairs through the village there were also lime trees, and the scent of lime blossom plus cowslip meadow was almost overpowering. The village drowsed in it; a solitary dog barked, a cuckoo called, nobody was about in the street or on the green.

"Quiet sort of place," Bill said, mopping his forehead. He parked the van on the grass verge and walked off towards the inn, the Fan-tailed Pheasant, pausing incredulously to stare at the sign. It depicted a pheasant with a most improbable tail, two feathers curved like a pair of washing-tongs.

Andrew picked up his microphone and looked about for material. A rhythmic thudding drew his eyes in the direction of a low wall. Beyond it lay a paddock shaded by walnut trees where a girl in shirt and jeans was schooling a pony. When the two men approached a wicket gate in the wall and stood by it, the rider trotted towards them inquiringly.

"Very photogenic," murmured Tod as his camera whirred. The girl was black-haired and her grey eyes seemed to reflect all the light from the sky; she was rather pale and had a long, graceful neck.

"Can I do something for you gentlemen?" she asked, dismounting from her pony.

"Excuse our troubling you—is this Midsummer Village?" Andrew asked.

"Certainly. Where else could it be?"

"You live here?"

"All my life, of course."

"Do you know that the village is up for sale, that the Trust which owns it is obliged to raise money by selling off this parcel of land?"

"Of course. Everybody in the village knows."

"And that the highest bid has come from Carrock, the millionaire, who has announced his intention, if he gets it, of turning it into a garden city?"

"Yes?" Her luminous eyes turned each of her responses to a question.

"Are you at all perturbed about this?" Andrew asked, slightly impatient at her lack of reaction.

"Perturbed." She turned the word over in her mind. "If I were at all perturbed," she said at last, "it would be for the man—Carrock. He is trying to buy a dream. He is bound to be disappointed."

Her pony tossed its head and snorted. She dropped the reins on its neck and let it go free.

"Of course you are familiar with the legend of Midsummer Village—that it is so beautiful it exists for only three days each year?"

"You were lucky in picking your day to come here, weren't you?" she said, and smiled slightly. He heard a little grunt of satisfaction, or anguish, from Tod with the camera.

"There must be some tale in the village to account for this belief," Andrew said. "Can you tell us?"

She leaned against the wall twirling a walnut leaf.

"Certainly. It originated in the eighteenth century when Morpurgo, the Poet Laureate, came to live here. He had been a fine poet, but by the time he became Laureate he was an old man. He slept all the year round and woke only for three days in the summer to compose an ode for the queen's birthday and earn his tun of wine. He had been crossed in love—in his youth he wanted to marry a beautiful girl called Laura who was so devoted to her twin brother that she had sworn she would never take a husband. Some say Morpurgo slept all year to forget his unappeasable grief. He was struck by lightning one summer day in his garden and died in his sleep."

"Did he never marry?"

"Oh yes, he married," the girl said rather scornfully. "He married a woman called Edith, a farmer's daughter thirty years younger than himself. As she had a smattering of witchcraft—nearly everyone knew a bit about it in those days—the tale goes that she put a spell on the whole place, that it should come alive only for three days every summer while Morpurgo was awake, writing his poem."

"Sleeping Beauty stuff," Tod muttered.

"And that is the legend of Midsummer Village?"

"That's the legend," the girl said, twirling her leaf. Then she threw it aside and clucked to the pony, which came to her willingly.

"Well, thank you very much," Andrew said, and they left her to her schooling, though both men looked back at her several times.

"Now who?" said Tod.

"Here's an old boy; looks like the squire."

An elderly man, upright, tall, and grey-headed, was approaching them.

"Might I trouble you for a few moments, sir?" Andrew inquired.

"By all means," said the man, though he gazed with a certain dislike at the camera and microphone.

"It's about this sale of Midsummer Village—have you any views on the matter, sir?"

"Naturally I have views," the elderly man said disdainfully, "though I doubt if they are of interest to the community at large. If this person, Carrock, who has the impertinent intention of buying our home, should care to pay us the common courtesy of a visit before completing his purchase, I shall be delighted to give him my views."

"Of course you are familiar with the legend of Midsummer Village?"

"Of course I am," the man said more graciously. "I shall relate it to you. It concerns a beautiful girl, the daughter of a farmer here in the valley. Both her parents died when she was in her teens, and she ran the farm single-handed."

"When did all this take place, excuse me, sir?"

"In the reign of Henry VIII. The girl, Edith, her name was, made a success of the farm. Her neighbours said the ghost of her father drifted beside her constantly, advising and instructing. No doubt he felt it was the least he could do, as he had made her promise not to marry."

"Why?"

"He came of a very old family, descended from the Danes, and he couldn't bear that the last of the line should change her name. He held her to her promise, though she was in love with a young man in the village. You can't argue with a ghost. She stayed single. She was famous for her butter and eggs, and her fine pigs and her cowslip wine. In any case it is doubtful if the man would have married her—he was considerably above her in birth and had a twin sister to whom he was very devoted."

"What became of the farmer's daughter?"

"In the end, oddly enough, a man came to live in the village who bore the same name as her father—and so, though she didn't love this man, she married him."

"Was he a poet?"

"I am hardly qualified to pronounce on that," the elderly man said fastidiously. "On her deathbed, after many years of married life—she was struck by lightning one summer day and died shortly after—it is said that Edith cried out: 'I have been alive only on three days in my life: the day I met him, the day he kissed me, and the day I lost him.' She was not referring to her husband. Since then, according to legend, the village exists for three days only in every year."

He looked round complacently at the lichened roofs and the towering elms. Grey cloud had begun to cover the sky, but on the village the sunlight still lay like concentrated gold.

"That's a most interesting tale, thank you, sir," Andrew said. The elderly man inclined his head slightly as they moved off with their equipment, and then he took a notebook from his pocket and strolled away, writing in it.

"Now who?" said Tod.

A woman was coming towards them. She carried a large basket of cowslips, and their colour was reflected in her massive coil of yellow hair.

She smiled at them in a friendly way and asked if she could help them, in a voice soothing and agreeable as the warmth from a baker's oven.

"We wondered if you'd care to give us your views on the sale of Midsummer Village?" Andrew said.

"Well, yon Carrock's on a fool's errand, isn't he?" she said, and laughed.

"Are you familiar with the legend of the village?"

"Of course," she said. "We're all brought up on it. My father used to tell it to me when I was a little thing. There was this young chap, Samuel Cutaway, oh, way back in the time of Henry the Seventh, he was to have been a monk but they dissolved the monasteries. Samuel fell in love with a farmer's daughter, but she hadn't any time for him. On account of this he went voyaging off with some of those early explorers and came back at the end of seven years with a pocket full of gold and a foreign bird. He became parish priest of the village here. He was a philosopher, he used to write essays. When he first heard the bird, in Africa it was, or maybe Australia, the song of it so bewitched him that he said while a man was listening to it he could explain the whole riddle of the universe. He brought the bird back with him. Some say it was a lyre bird, others a hoopoe."

"So did he explain the riddle of the universe?"

"He never got the chance," she said laughing. "The bird wouldn't sing in this cold climate, or only for the three hottest days every summer. Samuel took to drink, a gallon of cowslip wine every day in memory of the farmer's daughter who'd slighted him. And with every glass he drank he declared he would have been the greatest mind of his age if only the bird could be made to sing all the year round. So they say the village only exists now on the three days in summer when the bird would sing and he was listening to it and finding his answer to the riddle of the universe. If you'll excuse me, gentlemen, I must leave you now, I have to meet a friend."

"Thank you for your story," Andrew called after her as she hurried away.

"Here's the vicar," Tod muttered in his ear. "He's sure to be full of opinions." The vicar was a spare-looking man with a thin mouth, who gazed at them in faint disapproval while Andrew explained the reason for their presence.

"Have you any views on the sale of Midsummer Village, sir?"

"I? Views? Certainly. The Trust have no right to sell, Carrock has no right to buy. You should not sell times, or lives, or seasons."

"And the legend of the village—you know it, sir?"

"Naturally. It concerns a brother and sister who lived here in the reign of Charles the First."

"Twins?"

"Yes, twins. You know the tale?" the vicar said sharply.

But Andrew merely looked attentive, and so the vicar told his story. "This pair, Laura and Esmond Fitzroy, were so devoted to one another that they swore never to marry. But Esmond had a scientific bent and became more and more engrossed in studies until at last he retired to live in a tower—you may see it over there—" The vicar gestured towards a crumbling grey ruin among the beech woods. "His was a mind far in advance of his age. He achieved early discoveries in the uses of electricity, could make copper wires glow by magic, according to contemporary reports, and had a metal mast affixed to the roof of his tower, down which he received mysterious messages from celestial regions. The sister became jealous because he neglected her for his research—she was not intelligent, poor thing, merely had a talent for taming animals—so she put it about that he was in league with the devil. The villagers besieged him in his tower. He kept them at bay for three days—during which time he said he was receiving messages from on high telling him how to preserve the village for ever—and before they managed to drag him out there was a violent storm, and the tower was hit by lightning. Esmond, was killed and everybody said it was a judgment."

"What became of the sister? You said her name was Laura?"

"Oh, she married." The vicar dismissed her with brief contempt. "The legend goes that, out of revenge for his sister's betrayal, Esmond caused the village to disappear, and return for three days only each summer."

"That is extremely interesting, and thank you, sir," Andrew said.

"Glad to be of service." The vicar gave Andrew his card which was inscribed The Rev. S. E. Cutaway.

They left him and went along to drink cowslip wine at the Fan-Tailed Pheasant, where Bill was already enwreathed in more than a breathalyser's bouquet.

Coming out half an hour later they saw the fair-haired woman whom they had already met strolling towards them deep in conversation with a man in postman's uniform. She waved to them and, when they were within speaking distance, called:

"I forgot to tell you that he married."

"Who did? The philosopher with the singing bird?"

"Yes. He married, late in life, a girl who became so annoyed with his excuse of not being able to write unless the bird was singing that she swore she'd train it to sing all the time. She did, too. She had a way with animals."

"I suppose she also had a twin brother who died?"

"That's right, love. Well, I must be getting along to make my hubby's dinner. Good-bye Esmond, dear," said the fair-haired woman. She smiled at the postman and they kissed; she walked swiftly through a pair of large iron gates leading to a house among trees.

"And do you believe that this village exists on three days only each summer?" Andrew asked.

The postman, who was young and black-haired, grinned at him mockingly.

"I'd have an easy job if that was so, wouldn't I?" he said.

"But what do you think?"

"I'm not paid to think. I finished with thinking a long time ago."

With a casual flip of his hand, the postman walked off towards a small combined village store and sub-post-office.

"Well? What did my brother have to say?"

Andrew turned at the voice and saw the girl they had interviewed first.

"Have they told you some good stories?" she asked teasingly. "Shall you have to come back, do you think?"

"I—I'd like to," Andrew began uncertainly.

"Next time you come I'll show you my house, and my pets. But you have to pick your day, remember! Now I must hurry—there's going to be a storm."

"She's right," Tod said when she left them. "We'd best load up quick."

Andrew turned to look at the girl, who was entering a gate half-way along the village street. She waved her hand.

"Careful with the driving Bill," Tod said. "You're on the wrong side."

"Someone's greased the steering," Bill grumbled. "Listen: Don't they half have some songbirds in this village! What's that—a nightingale?"

"They sing louder when there's a storm on the way."

The van wove precariously along the village.

They were about half a mile beyond the last house, entering the beech woods, when lightning struck the bonnet.

When Andrew next opened his eyes, he was in a hospital bed, with a drip-feed attached to his arm.

"Are the others all right?" he asked, as soon as he was able to speak.

"Shock and concussion, that's all. You were all three lucky, considering the state of the van. Now, here's your father to see you, Mr Carrock—but he mustn't stay more than a few moments."

His father looked, as usual, prosperous, portly, and puzzled.

"Can't think why you have to gad about the country doing this ridiculous TV job," he grumbled. "If only you'd settle down and help me with the business, this kind of thing wouldn't happen. What's the matter with you—can't I give you everything you could possibly want?"

"Not quite," Andrew said, and smiled at his father weakly.

"Listen, Father—about that village you want to buy—can't I persuade you to change your mind?"

"Why?"

"It isn't the sort of place that ought to be bought."

"Matter of fact," said his father, "I don't need any persuading. Went to take a look at it—nothing there but a dip in the downs, some fields, and a lot of sheep. No houses. Not even ruins! Godforsaken spot. Forgotten all about it till you brought it up. Now, make haste and get better, my boy."

He gave his son an awkward, affectionate pat and hurried out.

Andrew lay thinking about a pair of luminous grey eyes.

"I wonder which story was the true one?" he mused. "I must ask Tod what he thinks."

But Tod and Bill had no theories to offer. Shock and concussion had taken away their memory of all events before the crash, and both of them persisted in declaring that they had never discovered the village at all.

The Helper

Paris in the rainy morning: like a series of triangles cut from pewter. The wet grey streets met one another at acute angles, shutters peered down slit-eyed, the town reflected a murky, watery sky. It was unfriendly, repulsing. Hostile.

Frost, consulting the professor's letter again—Charles-Edouard Aveyrand, Academician, 48 rue Lecluse—saw that he would not need to take a taxi or the metro; it would be an easy walk from the Gare St. Lazare. And he could do with a walk; he was hungry, stiff, and chilled to the bone from the night journey.

He ought to have remembered that address. And as he walked towards it, he did begin to remember.

"Knowing you to be an official of the British Patent Office," the professor had written in his formal stiff English, "and remembering our agreeable association of some years ago, I made bold to invite your assistance in this matter. My finances in these days are a matter of some anxiety, otherwise I would not have troubled you. My daughter Menispe invites herself to be recollected by you and regrets a lack of correspondence between the families since the sad death of your charming daughter."

Striding along the chilly canyon of a street, between high narrow grey houses and motorbikes that continually snarled at his elbow, Frost thought of Menispe Aveyrand. There was little need for her self-invitation, he thought. Only too easily could he summon up the image of the girl who, for five successive years, had come to stay en *famille* with the Frosts, learn English, and be, virtually, an adopted sister for Louise. Both girls had been only children; the arrangement, initiated through a school club, had proved so successful that when Menispe was not spending holidays in England, Louise went to the Aveyrand apartment in Paris.

Menispe at age nine had been a skinny waiflike little creature, all pale freckles and bony, sharp features, with an unexpectedly engaging triangular grin, a mobile face, never still for a moment, stringy fair hair, and shrewd hazel-green eyes. She was witty even then, *mechante*, but also touching; deprived of a mother since the age of six, she attached herself to the Frost family with passionate, starved affection, like a stray kitten offered its first bowl of warm milk. She and Louise had been inseparable, written each other immense weekly letters during the school terms, counted the days to each reunion. Frost and his wife had been "*chere tante* Josephine" and "*gentil oncle* Frank" in dozens of polite, dutiful breadand-butter letters always signed "*affectueusement, votre belle-fille,* Menispe."

The last visit, of course, had been that of Louise to the Paris apartment; after which, nothing more had been heard from Menispe.

Frost wondered, detachedly, how she had turned out. There had been a boyfriend, hadn't there, Lucien; what had become of him?

Perhaps she had married him.

The apartment house in which Professor Aveyrand lived was high, colourless, forbidding, with a mansard roof and so much exterior embellishment in the way of shutters, ironwork, lanterns, balconies, that there seemed hardly enough wall to sustain them. Inside, Frost remembered the varicose-veined marble and brown flock wallpaper, and the terrifyingly slow lift, with a heavy glass door, and room for only two persons inside, which creaked its way up from floor to floor.

It was in that lift that he had first been alone with his daughter Louise after the final visit, when he had come to fetch her home.

She had gazed away over his shoulder as if he did not exist, although they were obliged to stand almost pressed together. When he said, "I wonder what our chances are of getting a taxi?" she looked at him with the same total boredom as if he had speculated on the chances of the Tory candidate in the Stockton-on-Tees council elections.

Numero Onze, in trailing metal script on the door; the bell inside clanged at some distance, harshly, as he stood waiting in the close, windowless passage, only elbow-width, and lit by what appeared to be a three-watt bulb.

After a longish pause the door was opened by Professor Aveyrand himself. He had aged immensely since Frost's last visit; was gnarled, shaky, dwarfish, and stooped, like some ancient Nibelung creeping out of his crevice on the scent of gold. And that, Frost told himself sharply, was a thoroughly unfair judgment. The professor had always been the most abstracted, unworldly figure, plunged in the past and his studies; money was of no importance to him. Indeed, if he had not been so oblivious to what went on about him, of what his daughter was up to, at the time of that last visit, Frost might have been alerted a bit sooner, the calamity might never have happened . . . Enough of that.

By now the professor had gingerly, hesitantly, ushered him in. They were sitting on two upright chairs upholstered in hard brown velvet, facing one another across an empty marble hearth closed by a steel shutter. The apartment smelt dreadful—unaired, dusty, with a hint of something decaying—perhaps the plumbing needed attention, or a mouse had died in the pantry; it did not look as if the place ever, nowadays, received the attentions of a maid.

". . . since I retired had sufficient time to pursue my hobby," the professor was explaining—one thing, he had got down to business right away, no beating about the bush, there was that much to be said for him, thought Frost. Well, so much the better; who would want to spend an extra minute in this dank, depressing place with its horrible associations? "My family, of course . . . ," the professor went on.

"Interested in these matters for generations . . . Indeed an ancestor of mine in the sixteenth century . . . treatise on solar and planetary energy . . . as a matter of fact, he narrowly escaped execution for heresy . . ."

Frost dutifully·returned the old man's thin smile as he added, "Fortunately his patron was Cardinal Richelieu—the affair was smoothed over. He had to burn his books, of course, but . . . Before that . . . twelfth-century Sieur d'Aveyrand . . . brought back books on alchemy and physics from the East—and a wife too, a Moorish astrologer . . ."

"Indeed," Frost commented, politely concealing irritation and boredom. Now he remembered Menispe, aged twelve, airily boasting, "Of course I was named after a Saracen princess that one of our ancestors brought back from the Crusades. Don't you think it's rather *parvenu* not to know your family history?" "Snobbish little thing," he had teased her. "*Non, ce n'est pas snobbisme, oncle Frank, c'est pratique!*"

"What a very commendable record of your ancestors you have kept, Professor," he remarked. "I'm afraid in our family we can hardly trace our forebears beyond a pork butcher in 1893; but perhaps that is just as well. I daresay they were nothing to brag about."

The professor's pained, reluctant acknowledgment of this pleasantry made it evident that his views on the subject were widely divergent from those of Frost; he said, "Well, it is true . . . must be admitted that there are advantages . . . but now, let me show you my specifications."

He levered himself out of his chair—his arms looked as frail as celery stalks—and limped as fast as he was able to an Empire escritoire beside a lace-curtained window which looked into a dark interior well. The desk was piled high with papers which were plainly in no sort of order; it took the professor a little while to find what he wanted.

"Here, now—these, you see, are my diagrams—and these are the figures—it is all clear, I think, but my English is not adequate for the technical language—I do not know the proper terms for 'Unified Field theory' or 'planetary wave particle duality—" He had fallen into French, which Frost read and understood well, though he did not speak it with great fluency.

"Yes, I see, Professor. I don't think there will be any problem about that. Look, I have brought over some blank application forms. You fill them in like this—here, see—I will of course take care of the registration, and so forth—you will need a clear diagram of course; yes, this one should serve perfectly well. Put your name at the beginning, 'I, Charles-Edouard Aveyrand—'"

"De Froissart Aveyrand," put in the professor fussily.

"'Being a subject of the French Republic, do hereby declare the invention, for which I pray that a patent be granted to me, and the method by which it is to be performed, to be particularly described in and by the following statement—' Incidentally, do you have a made-up model of the—of your invention?"

"Naturally, Monsieur Frost, naturally I have."

To Frost's considerable surprise, he then lifted up his voice and called, "Carloman! Allo, Carloman!"

"I have programmed it to respond to my voice frequencies," he explained. "Of course, for another person, it would only be needed to slip in a different tape. All that is entered in the specification. I thought it most practical. I am, you see, sometimes very stiff with my rheumatic trouble, hardly able to rise from my chair; it is so with many of my age, I daresay: but the voice is always at command. *Bien*, here it comes; like its inventor, it does not move very fast."

A shuffling tread could now be heard in the corridor, and soon, round the open door, appeared a smallish figure, rather less than five foot high. Frost could not repress a start of surprise at the sight of it, for it appeared to be a knight in fourteenth-century armour. It moved slowly into the room and carefully positioned itself in the exact centre of a small threadbare rug about six feet away from the professor.

"Carloman, change the lights," ordered Aveyrand, and the model accordingly proceeded to shuffle slowly round the room altering the illumination; first it switched on various table lamps by pulling down their strings with its mailed hand; after this it turned off the switch by the door which governed the overhead light, encountering a little difficulty in getting its metal fingers on to the target; finally it switched off the standard lamp beside the professor's chair by pressing a floor switch with its mailed foot. Then it returned to the centre of the rug and stood, apparently awaiting further orders.

"Remarkable," said Frost. "Will it do anything else?"

"Oh, *bien sur*, but that is all I have programmed it for at present. Later it could be instructed to make beds, use the vacuum cleaner . . . But I thought, do you see, how useful for people who are afraid of thieves . . . I must confess I am often in anxiety about brigands breaking into this place and stealing my valuables when I am out." He glanced, almost apologetically over his shoulder. "One can leave the model, you see, with instructions to go round at irregular intervals of time, changing all the lights, so that it must appear some living person is there. A time switch could not be so irregular. Whereas I could give Carloman a random series of changes which would continue for one hundred days without repeating."

"Is it plugged into the mains? Or run off a battery?"

"Neither, monsieur; wholly self-contained. The planetary influence is sufficient to power it indefinitely on its present programme."

"Very clever indeed," said Frost. "I should certainly think you could find a ready market for such an invention."

"Oh, my dear sir! Without doubt! There are so many people who, like myself, fear thieves, fear to go away and leave their possessions."

Frost could not help being somewhat struck by the irony of this; looking round the dismal apartment he wondered what in it was worth taking? In any case, surely the professor was almost always at home?

"Tell me, why are you applying first for a British patent? Why not begin in your own country?"

The professor gave a classic Gallic shrug. "There is too much corruption here. I should have to grease too many palms. I cannot afford it. And otherwise, it would not be achieved in my lifetime, I would not reap the benefit . . . Although I am a sick old man, I still have some things left to offer the world—to render my name historic—this is only one of the uses of planetary energy which I propose."

A somewhat febrile glitter came into his eyes; he began muttering about Mars, Venus, and Saturn, until he was interrupted by a fit of coughing and obliged to stop, holding a soiled handkerchief to his lips. When the paroxysm went on and on, Frost, feeling that he ought to make some attempt at assistance, went into the next room, an indescribably sordid and untidy kitchenette. The sink was piled high with dirty dishes and there seemed nothing fit to eat or drink—not even a bottle of Evian water. However, the professor called out, "Coffee! Coffee!" in a feeble voice amid his eructations, and so Frost heated up a pan which contained mostly grounds and some discoloured liquid over the tiny gas stove, and brought a cupful of the stuff back to the old man. How could Louise have been so happy to spend so many holidays here? he wondered in amazed disgust, glancing round him. But of course that had been years ago, when the professor was still teaching at the Institute of Astronomy; there had been money enough for a *bonne* to help out in those days.

After drinking the gritty coffee, the professor in due course recovered sufficiently to complete the patent-application forms, which Frost then slipped into his briefcase.

"What do you call it, by the way? The invention has to have some sort of a title."

"I call it *l'Assistant*—the Helper."

"Would there be any chance of taking a—a specimen?" Frost then inquired. "To England, I mean? It might facilitate—speed up the process, you know—if I could present a model as well as the drawings. Do you, perhaps, have others?"

"Other models? *Non, non*—Carloman *seulement,*" the professor replied, after looking vaguely round the room, as if there might possibly be another, somewhere, only just at present his memory failed him regarding its whereabouts. He added, after a moment, "I suppose you might perhaps take that one; doubtless I could construct another without too much trouble."

"Why did you make it in the form of a crusader?" Frost asked. He looked with dislike at the motionless figure on the rug; it filled him with a slight, uneasy feeling of repugnance. He had always been annoyed by phoney antiquity, cigarette lighters in the shape of jousting knights, mock-baronial coalscuttles—he found Carloman in decidedly poor taste.

"Why in that shape? Oh, merely because I happened to have the armour. There were various pieces left from the collection in our family chateau—now sold, alas, to foreigners. But possessing the armour already saved me some tedious construction work. Also it is convenient—*regardez*—" Aveyrand flipped up Carloman's visor and revealed a mass of wires and connections where the face should have been. He added absently. "I do have other pieces of armour, *bien sur,* I would be able to construct another model. It is just that I am so pressed for time." He reflected. "Carloman is not too heavy. We could, I daresay, pack him into a golf bag. Somewhere, I will recollect in a moment, there used to be such an article. Thus you might carry it back to England."

"Perhaps I could help you find the bag?"

Frost glanced around the overfurnished room. The sooner he was out of this dreary place, the better.

"*Merci, mon ami.*" The professor rubbed his forehead uncertainly. "It might be on top of the armoire in my bedroom . . . You forgive that I do not accompany you? I have to husband my strength these days."

Passing a couple of rooms rammed to the ceiling with the accretions of years—from which he nervously averted his eyes—Frost searched in the bedroom's dusty disorder, and did, after a while, manage to unearth the golf bag among a stack of photographic equipment, rucksacks, telescopes, botanical specimen cases, and aged wicker luggage. On a chiffonier he was disconcerted to encounter a photograph of his daughter Louise and her friend Menispe, arm in arm, laughing and squinting into the sunshine of a Paris street; from this he hastily averted his eyes. He left the bedroom and carried the bag back into the *salle*.

Aided rather ineffectually by the professor, who, by the end of the interview, very evidently had little energy to spare, Frost managed to pack the armour-suited model into the golf bag, wadding it with copies of *Le Monde* and *France Soir*. "What about the programming?" he thought to ask. "It will need your voice, won't it?"

"There is a tape built in—no problem. You merely move the switch to the second position—*voilà*—to re-record."

"Yes, yes, of course. Well, I will say good-bye, Professor—I'm sure I have tired you long enough. It has been extremely interesting—"

"I regret infinitely that I cannot offer you *dejeuner*—but the resources of my kitchen these days are so limited, I go out so seldom—"

"No, no, my dear sir—don't think of such a thing—" Frost suppressed a shudder as he thought of that kitchen.

"I am deeply sorry, also, that my daughter Menispe did not return in time to see you again."

"Menispe? You mean that she is still living here?" Frost was not sure why this information startled him so. Menispe had not seemed the kind of daughter who would remain under the parental roof a day longer than she was obliged to. He recalled that last occasion; her all-too-evident boredom and scorn . . .

"But of course she still lives here!" The professor seemed quite shocked. "Who, if not she, my daughter, would look after me and charge herself with my errands?"

Although Frost entertained no very kind feelings towards Menispe, he could not avoid a shiver at this calm statement by her father.

What a fate for the wretched girl, he thought, and he asked, "Did she not marry, then? What became of her fiancé—Lucien, was it?"

"Ah, Lucien? Poor young man, he died, some years ago. He contracted an unfortunate addiction—"

Like Louise. Frost found himself inquiring dispassionately, "Menispe herself never did so?"

"No, monsieur. Menispe is not liable to such habits."

No. She merely observes the results of them in her friends, Frost thought, but Aveyrand continued, "She has problems, though, she will not eat enough—sometimes I am very disquieted about her. Ah, but—*a la bonheur*—there she comes now!" he exclaimed in a tone of triumph as the outer door rattled.

Frost let out a silent, heartfelt oath. In all the world the last person he wanted to see was Menispe Aveyrand; if only he had cut short his visit by five minutes, this encounter could have been avoided.

Now she came strolling in with a faint smile, lifting her chin, staring at him impudently under lowered sandy eyelashes; they might have met five minutes before, instead of seven years. She was wet through from the rain which was beating down in earnest now, but seemed unaware of the fact; she did not remove her outer clothes for she had none to take off, her garments consisting of worn jeans, thong sandals, and a draggled Indian shirt. Her hair was close-cropped, and her face resembled that of some starving waterbird—she was skeleton-thin, seemed smaller, if possible, than in those bygone days when she had come to stay in Wimbledon.

"Menispe!"

He could not be cordial, his tongue refused the hypocritical forms of greeting, all that he could muster, lamely enough, was, "Fancy seeing you again."

"Monsieur Frost—what a surprise!" Her tone was ironic, she did not seem in the least surprised. She slung a leg over the scrolled end of a dusty green velvet chaise-longue, and sat watching him with a slight smile as he gathered together the handles of the golf bag.

"What, you are taking away our poor Carloman? Kidnapping him? Shall we never see him again?"

"It is very kind of Monsieur Frost to interest himself in our affairs," her father said repressively. "Considering—"

"Considering?" Menispe lit a thin brown cigarette and blew a smoke-ring. "Considering that his wife and daughter are dead? Monsieur Frost probably has time on his hands."

"Menispe! Monsieur Frost kindly undertakes the English patent for us."

"So; soon, then, we shall be rich?"

"I hope so," Frost said coldly. "Of course you can never tell whether these things will get taken up by manufacturers."

Now he was overcome by weary distaste for the whole project. Why should he take any pains to enrich this hateful pair? In any case, Aveyrand looked to be at death's door, would probably go off within the next year or so, while his daughter seemed like a cadaver as it was. And then—to remember Louise. With all her happy intelligence, her bright promise cut short—

"I will write to you from London as soon as I have any news," Frost said hastily to the Professor, and manoeuvred himself and his burden awkwardly out of the door.

"Do not let Carloman get rusty!" Menispe called after him.

Going down in the lift—he had to hold Carloman vertically in order to fit him in—Frost was reminded again of Louise by the question of whether he would be able to find a taxi.

Back at his cottage in Essex—for he had left Wimbledon after the death of Louise and his wife's subsequent suicide—he did not immediately unpack the bag containing Aveyrand's model. There was plenty to do after a three-day absence—the house needed cleaning, the lawn had grown shaggy. And on the following morning at the Patent Office, he found his desk piled high with accumulated work which would require several days to clear.

Nevertheless, it was not the outcome of will, of premeditated plan, his slowness to take action on Aveyrand's behalf. He had sincerely meant to respond to the old man's appeal for help. When he decided to go to Paris, his intentions had been disinterested and benevolent; he felt it was not his business to make judgments or withhold professional advice when it was requested.

But now . . . All he could feel was a profound lethargy and reluctance. No doubt the profits from the manufacture and marketing of Carloman's issue would in time earn the old man—and Menispe—a considerable amount of money. What would they do with it? That was no affair of Frost's.

He asked himself once or twice why he did not simply turn the professor's application over to a colleague to deal with—that would be the rational solution to his problem. But still, day after day, he let the papers lie on his desk, and for some weeks Carloman remained zipped into the golf bag under the copies of *France Soir.*

Nearly four months after his trip to Paris, Frost received an Eiffel Tower card addressed to him in a familiar looped untidy black handwriting.

"My father has asked me to inquire if there is any news of his patent," wrote Menispe—no "*cher Oncle Frank*" this time. "He grows discouraged at your long silence and would be pleased to receive a letter from you."

Prompted by this, guilty and resentful, Frost unpacked the model and set it up. Winter had come with promise of snow, and several lights were burning in his cottage. Following the professor's instructions, Frost re-recorded the tape, slotted it back into the visor, and then, clearing his throat, feeling somewhat foolish, he ordered the model:

"Carloman, change the lights."

Obediently the model began moving about Frost's living room, switching on any lights that were off, and turning off those that were already on; evidently this was its all-purpose programme if not provided with more specific instructions. Its movements were slow, fumbling and hesitant, as it worked over this new course, but thorough. When the lights were all changed, it returned to the spot where it had first stood, and took up its position there, motionless, waiting.

"All right, Frankenstein, that's enough," muttered Frost, with a slight shiver—there was something disagreeably like Aveyrand himself about the model's uncertain, cautious movements—and he hastily clicked off the master switch on the breastplate.

"I'll put the application in today," he resolved.

That day was unusually harassed, though; and on the following morning he received a long letter from a friend in Australia, a distant cousin of his wife, who by some mischance had never been informed of her death and proposed visiting England next month; that necessitated a long letter going through, yet again, the whole miserable story of how, following the death of Louise from an overdose, Mary had sunk into such a deep depression that one night when Frost was kept late at the office by a rush of work she had decided to end it all . . .

By the time he had finished his letter, Frost was feeling so bitterly hostile towards the Aveyrand family that he deliberately decided to put aside the professor's application for another month. He could not, he simply *could not* take any action about it just at present. Why should he be the one to act for them? Let them wait a little longer.

And a month later his eye was caught by a small paragraph in the *Times* as he travelled home one evening: "French Academician dies. Charles-Edouard Aveyrand, for many years Professor in Astrophysics at the Paris Faculté des Sciences . . . author of *La Revolution Astrophysique, Opuscules Astronomiques, Employant Venus et Saturne*, etc., etc. . . . holder of the following academic honours and decorations . . . was found dead in his Paris apartment yesterday. He lived alone, having been predeceased by his daughter, who had died in hospital of anorexia nervosa two weeks before. By a sad piece of irony, the professor, too, it is thought, died of undernourishment and hypothermia. Neighbours were alerted to his fate because the lights in his apartment remained on day and night for a week."

So: he never made that second model, thought Frost, after a blank, shocked moment. If he had, perhaps the neighbours would not have found him yet; Carloman II would still be stumping about the apartment, switching lights on and off at random intervals.

He re-read the paragraph, waiting for guilt and remorse to bite. But all he felt was a kind of dreary satisfaction; even guilt seemed wasted on that pair. Aveyrand would hardly have lasted much longer, with all the wealth in the world; nor would Menispe, and it was unlikely that anybody regretted her passing.

But what, now, should he do with Aveyrand's invention? Enter the patent in his own name and give the proceeds to charity? Search for other family connections? Or—his strongest impulse—do nothing, smash the model to smithereens with a hatchet?

The train pulled up at his station. He put the *Times* in his briefcase, got out, and walked up the long and muddy lane towards his cottage.

Yes: a hatchet might be the best solution to Carloman. On the other hand—he might just keep the model, which was proving quite useful. There had been a number of burglaries lately in the district; he had formed the habit of leaving Carloman switched on, to create the effect of human activity in the house.

Indeed the lights changed as Frost approached the cottage: the kitchen window went dark and, after a short interval, the bedroom was illuminated. Handy though the model was, Frost thought, opening the gate, it was hard to conquer the slight unease of entering the house, aware that somewhere inside this mindless but human-seeming object was plodding slowly around, carrying out its programmed tasks.

Then, glancing through the window of the ground-floor bedroom, Frost was startled to observe that, this evening, Carloman had performed a task for which he had not yet been programmed: he was just moving away from the bed, having, with his gauntleted hands, twitched back the covers.

With a suddenly accelerated heart, and a dry mouth, Frost opened the front door, which led straight into the dining room. The table was laid for two.

Now he could hear slow, thudding steps as the model negotiated the short passage from bedroom to hall. Soon the thing came in sight, moving deliberately with its slow, swaying gait. The closed bars of the visor looked straight ahead: blind, expressionless. But inside them—Frost was visited by a mad notion—inside, if he were to lift the visor, he believed that he would reveal not a random-seeming mass of wires and terminals but the mocking, hostile features of Menispe Aveyrand.

The Monkey's Wedding

☆ ☆
☆

FAMOUS PICTURE DISCOVERED AFTER FIFTY YEARS: said the headlines. *The Monkey's Wedding* located at last. And, underneath, in smaller type, the newspaper stories told how Jan Invach's celebrated, almost legendary picture of a street scene in the town of Rocjau, the people in the street, the man running with the dove, the girl with red hair, and the high-arched, 700-year-old bridge over the river Fos—well, anyway, this wonderful picture, which had sold on its first showing for £8,000, and that was in 1939, and soon after, in World War II, it had been lost in France, looted by the Germans, taken to Berlin, looted again by the Russians, taken to Moscow, lost again, and had only recently come to light after having been smuggled over the frontier between Kikl and Soubctavia. Well, this historic picture had now been reclaimed by its painter, Jan Invach, who had made a special journey to Soubctavia (now torn asunder, alas, by disastrous civil war and dire internal strife) to identify the painting, of which, since it was lost, he had done two more versions from memory, but had always wished to recover the original if it were possible to do so. "The Monkey's Wedding" of course, in colloquial idiom, means a scene with sunshine viewed through rain, or rain seen through the sun's rays. Jan Invach painted the original picture at the age of eighteen. Now in his 70s but hale and well, he is world-famous and his pictures fetch astronomic sums. What *The Monkey's Wedding* first version must be worth now is almost impossible to compute . . .

Old Mrs Invach sniffed, reading this news story as related by various daily papers while drinking elderflower tea in her large, dark, shabby, cluttered Hampstead kitchen.

"Untold millions, ha! Money's not worth the paper it's printed on these days. In 1939, with what that picture sold for, you could have bought a couple of islands. Now you couldn't buy a tub of ice cream. And if you could, it wouldn't be worth eating."

Old Mrs Invach, now in her 90s, talked to herself all day long. It was a family habit. Her son did it as he painted his pictures. Sitters for portraits were frequently disconcerted, and sometimes tried to respond, but he paid them no heed. The Tate Gallery had a tape of the entire monologue that had accompanied his charcoal drawing of the Duchess of Cambridge.

"United Nations monitoring a cease-fire in Soubctavia. Ha! That won't last long! I know those Soubs and those Dobrindjans—they'll be at each other's throats again in thirty-six hours."

There were shots of the beautiful old town of Rocjau and the celebrated bridge—now shattered beyond repair, nothing left of its 700-year-old curve but some dangling fragments of masonry.

"If they ever want to rebuild it, they'll need to look at Jan's picture," muttered Mrs Invach. "But will that time ever come? I very much doubt it."

"The world-famous painter Jan Invach is in the town of Rocjau at present, on a mission to rescue his legendary picture *The Monkey's Wedding* which was recently discovered not far away in a barn, just over the border in the province of Kikl. An unknown sum had been paid for its ransom by an unknown Japanese millionaire who wished to return the picture to the man who painted it. He plans to donate it to the National Gallery in London, but before that he intends to effect various necessary repairs to the canvas, which was discovered leaning against a damp wall behind a heap of turnips . . .

"A threatened strike of dentists has been averted by the junior Health Minister . . ."

The doorbell rang, and Mrs Invach switched off the weather forecast and shuffled into the front hall, muttering and grumbling. It took her a while to undo various bolts and Chubb locks; the chain she left on while she peered round the crack of the door into the face of a lad of perhaps eighteen who wore a brand-new tartan cap and carried a shiny briefcase.

"Evening, missus!" he said with cheerful confidence. "I represent McCustody home security systems and burglar alarms. I'll be happy to survey your home here and now, and give you a free estimate for our complete scheme of protection—"

He was studying her intently all the time as he spoke, and she, meanwhile, was subjecting him to en equally gimlet-eyed scrutiny. Mrs Invach was a rugged-looking old lady with hair and skin almost completely pale, bleached as desert grass; her scanty hair was pulled straight back into a knot, she wore a rough woollen monk's robe, and her eyes were like flint arrowheads.

"Why should you think I haven't a security system already?" she demanded tartly.

"I checked round with all the main companies before I came." The boy gave her a brash grin. "None had your name on their lists. And, just now, you'll be wanting a fair deal of extra security—won't you?"

"What do you mean by that?" she snapped.

Somehow, during this exchange, she had moved back a step or two, and he had contrived to twitch off the doorchain and enter her front hall, which he glanced round, taking rapid stock of its solid walls and massive Victorian mahogany stair rail. When he raised his eyes to the upper level he drew in a sharp breath, for there, facing each other across the stair head, were two Jan Invach paintings, explosions of dark, brilliant, menacing colour.

"When your son comes back to England with that picture," he said with a candid grin.

"What do you know about my son?" the old woman demanded.

"I read the papers, don't I? My firm expects me to scout about, finding likely customers. You want all the art thieves in Europe making a beeline for this house? Now, we can put you in a foolproof, sabotage-resistant, easy-care system *exactly* suited to your needs"—he tapped his fat briefcase—"in less than twenty-four hours; you can have it all installed and be able to snap your fingers at bandits."

He snapped his fingers.

"All I need is to take a look at your ground-floor rooms—" He glanced with unconcealed inquisitiveness towards the two doors—drawing room, dining room, most probably, which opened on either side of the hall, and the third door at the rear, leading, no doubt, to the kitchen regions.

But Mrs Invach wasn't having any.

"No. Thank you, young man. Not today. Not any day, for that matter. I do not need your security system, or anybody's. I take my own measures. Thank you. Good day."

She pushed him inexorably back through the crack of the door.

"You'll be sorry—really sorry! You don't know what a bad mistake you are making," he called back through the crack.

"I make my own mistakes!" she shouted. After re-locking the door behind him she moved slowly towards the kitchen to prepare her evening meal. On the dark-blue kitchen walls above the dirty braided rug glimmered half a dozen more Invach canvases, some framed, some unframed. The kitchen was roomy and dim, with a pot-bellied iron stove, a large old refrigerator, and a small Victorian bureau used by Mrs Invach as a bar, containing bottles of vodka, bourbon, bitters, wines, and liqueurs. Racks of tapes hung on one wall, and the old woman switched on a player as she mixed herself a drink, cut up onions, and chopped spinach.

Her son's voice filled the room, arguing with itself in a low, collected murmuring monologue just louder than a whisper.

"Sky's getting darker now—float of azure mist against distant hill—smoke rolling up from somebody's bonfire—'commentary-driving' they used to make you do it on those advanced motor courses, opposing traffic, hazards, mirror, say I'm doing a moderate thirty in a built-up area—lemon-green in the ash flowers, splash of white on top of that mushroom shape, loose flecks of black in the angle—now there's a woman walking along, throws up her feet like serifs on capital letters, put her in, back like a stick of celery just what I need, a vertical up there hooking into the sky—great wallop of white cloud like a walrus's back arching up over the house tops—houses climbing the hill make a dark diagonal—something coming towards me, green on lighter green—"

Mrs Invach sighed and dropped her vegetables into a pot to sizzle and frizzle in oil. Later she would add milk and stock. She lived almost entirely on vegetable soup. Up above her in the gloom she heard a faint keening whistle.

"All right, all right," she grumbled. "I got your bones, don't worry."

Some of the bones had gone into her soup stock, but some remained raw as a snack for Alpha and Beta, the two peregrines, who had their own entry in a round, east-facing window upstairs, their home in a dark cobwebby loft.

"Texture very important," said her son's voice. "And everything must be three-dimensional. Except the sky? Even the sky? Can you have three-dimensional sky? Don't see why not. What else is there besides up, across, and sideways? Before? After? Alongside? Next door? Now, in that mass of black a red sun hanging—it needs to pierce the black like blood soaking through a bandage . . . Black must have texture, though, solid as rock all criss-crossed and veined with seams of fine, very dark brown . . . But the red comes clear through, round as a penny . . ."

Presently Mrs Invach went upstairs to bed. Her bedroom was virtually empty, save for the large flat bed, like a platform, covered by a Turkish rug and cushions. Inside the bedroom door a massive vacuum cleaner attached to the wall by a tangle of tubes and cords. On three walls, more of Jan's pictures, severe, complex, and luminous. The fourth wall held two huge windows, oblong against blackness, with wide low sills.

Before her final descent into bed, Mrs Invach regularly devoted the last hour of her day to what she called "searching."

The first stage was a physical search for all the items she had mislaid in the course of the day, in the course of the week: she lived in permanent arrears, carried out a nonstop quest for her scarf, her spectacles, the gas bill, the book she was reading, another book now due for return to the library, a letter from Cousin Anatol in Buffalo, her favourite pen, her membership card of the Foreigners' Forum, an advertisement for Arthritis Oil, a newspaper clipping she intended to send to her niece in Tokyo, a packet of plant food, a scented candle somebody had given her which was supposed to be a specific against insomnia, an invitation to a private view of watercolours, a letter long overdue for an answer from a man who wanted to write her biography, and keys, dozens of keys . . . All these things needed to be found, and some of them, perhaps, would be found, but then, most probably, lost again in the hunt for others which were, or seemed, more instantly necessary.

And some would never be found.

The retrieval of even one, even two lost possessions would quickly operate a change of gear in Mrs Invach's mental workings: she would steady down, restlessness replaced by an inward-looking process; she sat herself comfortably on the broad bedroom windowsill where found objects were first laid (before being lost again) and began to operate her majestic memory. The contents of her mind, a huge lumber room containing ninety years of accumulated events, were like an archaeologist's treasure heap, like the buried cities of Troy. Into this heap she plunged a scoop and dragged out whatever she fancied. If only it could be so with the things in the house!

"Nineteen forty-one. Jan and I walking across Europe, dodging the Germans. The night we spent with Professor Crzvdgrad and talked about rainbows—then next day they caught him, arrested him, and put him in a camp. We heard of his death four years later . . . And it was on that walk that Jan painted the first *Monkey's Wedding;* he carried it with him, rolled in his sleeping bag. I remember the man with the dove . . ."

The telephone rang, insistently. Sifting back into shadows, the man with the dove returrned to the year 1941. Mrs Invach had a phone extension on the bedroom windowsill. She picked up the receiver.

"Mrs Ludmila Invach? This is Sam Stoles of the *Morning Post* art page. I understand you were with your son Jan when he painted the original *Monkey's Wedding* picture—when you were escaping from German-occupied Europe?"

"I was with him," growled Mrs Invach. She detested newspapers and newspapermen but knew that it was not wise to antagonize them.

"You watched him paint the picture?"

"Oh, not all the time. It took him six days, you know."

"Six days of great danger when the Germans were coming closer and closer."

"You don't have to tell me that, young man."

"You have heard that he has retrieved the picture—is coming back to this country with it?"

"So the gossip runs—"

"Will he be coming to your house?"

"Possibly. I have not yet been informed. Perhaps he will take it straight to the National Gallery—to work on it there—"

So said Mrs Invach, but in fact she believed that Jan would come to Hampstead. Why not? In between his huge travels he generally did use her big top-floor studio.

"Your son has a home of his own? Is he married? Children?"

"No. Never. None."

"And his father? Your—husband?"

"Gone. Long ago. He remained behind in Dobrin. Died, I heard, when Jan was ten." These facts came from Mrs Invach like dregs of juice from an already-squeezed lemon.

"Young man, I am at this time expecting my son to telephone me. I would be much obliged if you would hang up. I can tell you no more. Good night."

"Good night, Mrs Invach."

She was not expecting her son to call, but in fact two minutes later the phone did ring again, a foreign operator asked a question.

"Pirhda? Ach—Jan, it is you! From where do you call?"

"Mother? I'm in Rocjau—in a callbox. Listen: things are quite rough here. Can you hear the gunfire?"

She could, like a spatter of hail against the windows. But it was June . . .

"They have snipers in the hills around, firing into the town, teasing the inhabitants . . . They watch a woman go to the well with her pail, they wait until she has returned within three steps of her front door, then drill a row of holes into the pail . . ."

That was so like Jan; he paid heed only to the inessentials, the small details.

"But did you get the picture? When can you come back here?"

"Yes, I got the picture. Mother, do you remember a girl called Amalcja? In Rocjau?"

Down plunged the accurate probe into the mass of memories.

"Certainly I remember her." A girl with brilliant red hair and a brilliant razor-sharp mind. A combative, scrutinizing girl. A rival. "She died in a camp, we heard."

"No," said Jan. "She did not die. Not then, not there."

"So? Is that so?" Mrs Invach playing for time.

"You were wrong when you told me that, Mother."

Did he mean *wrong* in the moral sense, or merely mistaken?

She said, evasively, "So many untrue stories ran about at that time. You have news of her?"

"No, only that she did not die. She—"

"But when will you come back?"

"Tomorrow, if I can make it to the U.N. headquarters. If we can make it to the airport. They call that road Suicides' Mile."

"I wish that you were here, now," she said, sounding, suddenly, her full age, and pitiful. "*Why* did you have to go back for that picture? It was lost for so long—"

"It was a part of me. I needed to take another look. Good-bye, Mother!"

"I shall see you back in London!" she called loudly, but the line had already gone dead, and she was left with the empty receiver in her hand, staring across a wide, dangerous distance in which a red-haired girl—not handsome, no, but with a keen scornful face like the prow of a ship—a redheaded girl had laughed and argued and teased, and made far too strong a bid for her son Jan's attention.

Next day Mrs Invach got up very late and shuffled around the house all day in her threadbare monk's robe and Turkish slippers. For once, the house was quite silent. She had not the heart to talk to herself, she did not dare play tapes of Jan's voice. That would be to tempt the wicked spirits. And there were far too many of those about the world, too many and too strong. Some of them inside herself.

What had happened to that girl Amalcja? Where had she gone? What had she done with herself?

We were happy, thought Mrs Invach, just the two of us, until she came along. Some men—the great artists—are better alone. They do not need women. Art is enough for them. Jan was one of that sort.

Was? What do I mean by was? Perhaps he is coming in to Heathrow at this moment.

But at tea-time—not that Mrs Invach drank tea; she drank vodka with homemade elderflower cordial, made from her own backyard trees—the Foreign Office South-Eastern Europe Cultural and Educational Department rang her.

"Mrs Invach?"

"Yes," she croaked, knowing already.

"We are sorry to bring you bad news—"

"Yes?"

"Your son—the painter Jan Invach—he has been very seriously wounded, on his way to the airport at Rocjau. He was flown out—to Ancona—where he is in a hospital, in intensive care—but hopes for his survival are not high. We think it best to warn you—"

"Should I go there? To Ancona? Should I get on a plane?"

"No, no, Mrs Invach, we cannot advise that. No, but what we are calling to inquire is—"

"Yes? Yes?"

"The painting your son went to verify—to establish—to authenticate—"

"So?"

"He had it with him when he was—it has been despatched to this country. There were some bullet holes and a tear—nothing too bad—"

"The picture is okay but my son is dying?" sourly said Mrs Invach.

"The picture will be delivered to you *very shortly,* Mrs Invach. This was at your son's express request. He would not rest until he was assured that it was on its way. We would like to arrange for police protection of your house during the next five days, Mrs Invach—we have made arrangements with the Art and Antiques squad at Scotland Yard—until acknowledgment of the legal ownership of the picture has been definitely established—"

"*Established?*" she spat.

"It is a matter for knotty legal consideration, Mrs Invach. The Japanese buyer who acquired it—he made it plain that his intention was to give it to your son—give it back to him—"

"Give it back? But my son painted it in the first place. It was his, his own work, his property—"

"Not so, Mrs Invach, for he sold it—the original purchaser is lost, unavailable. But the question is, did the Japanese gentleman have the right to buy it—for it had been stolen, several times—"

"It belongs to my son!"

"And suppose your son should not survive, Mrs Invach?"

She said: "Excuse me. Somebody is ringing at my front door bell. I must hang up."

"*Mrs Invach!*"

She put back the receiver on its rest and pattered to the front door. There a delivery man handed her a rolled-up package three metres long, lavishly wrapped in plastic wadding, secured with heavy tape and gaudy labels and numerous lead seals.

She was asked to sign in nine different places.

The delivery man drove off, having first subjected the house, in its untidy garden, to a long, careful scrutiny.

Mrs Invach shut, bolted, and chained the front door. Carrying the package through to the kitchen she began tussling with the formidable wrappings. Kitchen scissors and a razor blade at last defeated them. She took the rolled canvas into what had once been the dining room. Now the huge mahogany table, bloomed over with damp, held old maps, boxes of family papers, rolls of patchwork, an old-fashioned wind-up gramophone, and a Singer sewing machine, period 1890.

All these things were thrust onto the floor, and the canvas unrolled, weighted down at the corners with large lumps of rock brought home from the Dolomite Mountains.

The Monkey's Wedding blazed up at the ceiling, and Mrs Invach stood, hands on hips, a crease between her brows, estimating what must be done to it. The bullet holes, there and there, yes, a dark stain of blood, and patches of damp—from the turnip-heap, probably—and a tear, quite a bad tear at one corner . . .

Sombrely, lower lip outthrust, frowning still, she left the room, head bent. She locked the dining-room door and put the key in her skirt pocket. Went to watch the six o'clock news.

"The well-known painter, Jan Invach, died of bullet wounds this afternoon in a military hospital in Ancona after a successful bid to rescue his world-famous picture *The Monkey's Wedding* from the war-torn town of Rocjau. The painting is now on its way to the National Gallery in London, where . . ."

Is it, though? thought Mrs Invach, scowling, switching off the TV set. I'd like to see them get their hands on it before I come to a decision about it.

She ate her soup and conducted her evening search, more random than usual, but triumphantly unearthing a set of croquet mallets and an album full of Siberian stamps. Then she went to bed, after feeding the peregrines. But in the middle of the night they woke her, keening and mewing in the darkness of her bedroom.

"What is it, what's to do?" she demanded.

And was answered by a frantic cry from the floor, somewhere near her bed.

"Murder, *murder*, they're killing me, they're digging their claws into my brain! Make them get off, make them let go of me! Arrgh, you brutes, you monsters!"

Both birds had settled firmly onto the head of someone who had been crawling towards the bed from the doorway: beaks and talons were embedded in his scalp. Mrs Invach observed the situation in the dim starlight from the huge windows, and smiled grimly.

"How did you get in? Oliver Twist? Eh?"

"Through the round window—they'll blind me—it's torture—oh, please, please!"

"Have you accomplices outside?"

"Yes, in a truck, waiting till I'd pierced the gas capsule and let them in—"

"A gas capsule, huh? Where is that, then?"

It was in his limp hand, already broken. Mrs Invach, without comment, smashed a window with the croquet mallet and switched on the vacuum cleaner to blow instead of suck.

Then she called the police art-theft squad on the special radio line which they had insisted on installing when she refused conventional protection.

"I have a truck full of thieves in my garden. Can you take them away?"

"What about me?" whimpered the defeated figure on the floor. "For pity's sake, make these monsters leave go of me."

"You be quiet," she said, "or I'll order them to peck your eyes out."

He fell silent.

Police arrived like lightning, swarming over the garden, seizing the truck and its occupants. But Mrs Invach utterly refused to let them into the house.

"I have my own security system, thank you very much!" she snapped at the sergeant.

After they had gone with their captives, leaving four men on guard outside, Mrs Invach returned to her bedroom and ordered the peregrines to let go of their prey. He struggled to his knees, very dejected, rubbing fingers gingerly through his rumpled red hair. His tartan cap had fallen off onto the mat.

"Well, Oliver Twist?" repeated Mrs Invach sourly. "What have you got to say for yourself?"

He was the boy from McCustody Security.

"I—I thought it would be a good way to get into the house—see the pictures—that was why I got in touch with them—because I'm small—could get through the round hole—"

He gave her a defeated, hangdog look.

"I know who you are," said Mrs Invach after a long, long pause. "You are Amalcja Kodan's son."

He nodded, then shook his head. "No, her grandson. Anatol."

"Where are they? Your mother? Your grandmother?"

"Dead. Both."

"Ah, so," she said. "So I was right in that, at least."

The boy stared at her uncomprehendingly. "My mother died five years ago. She said—she was always saying—that I should see my grandfather—get in touch—"

The old woman sniffed.

"Why should he want to see you? What use could you be to him?"

Anatol stiffened defensively.

"I am a painter, too!"

"Ha! You? At—how old are you?"

"Eighteen. And I have studied. And I know how to restore canvases—I am an expert—"

At eighteen? At eighteen, she thought, Jan was well under way. But this boy?

"What I wanted—but what I really wanted," he said, "was to hear the tapes. All those tapes you have. I read about them in the paper. My grandfather, talking as he painted. Well, I wanted to meet him, of course. That was why—it took a long time to get to this country."

"It would not have been any use, your seeing him," she said. "He never talked to anybody. Not really. But the tapes—"

Drawing in a sharp breath, she switched on the player in her bedroom.

". . . clouds like piano keys; shine of water in the shadow dark green and thick like sump oil—tree full of white eyes, each one looking a different way—hand sunk in the fur, very solid, reddish, artisan's hand, thick with bone—not at all like my hands, mine long and skinny, skeleton's hands very nearly—like the old girl's hands, hers on the way to skeleton, her face colour of bleached mummy—now, touch of dark red here, stroke it on—yellow-green light moving towards saffron . . ."

She had switched on the light. She saw the boy had angry tears in his eyes. "Why couldn't I meet him?"

"He's dead."

"I know. I heard on my transistor."

"But I have all the tapes here. And a lot of the pictures."

Mrs Invach took stock of the boy, measuring him grimly. "Well, you can come here and listen to the tapes, I suppose. If you like."

His eyes blazed.

"Yes! And can I see *The Monkey's Wedding*?"

"Very well."

She led the way downstairs to the dining room, where the picture still lay spread out on the massive old table. She switched on all the lights and heard a policeman cough and stamp outside.

The boy began to walk slowly round the table, round and round, stooping sometimes, with his face close to the surface, to peer at a crack, or a bullet hole, or a bloodstain, never quite touching the canvas, but his eyes almost stroking it, his hands making small, blind, fluttering movements, as if they held invisible tools.

Old Mrs Invach, perched on a high stool, watched him.

As he walked round and round, back and forth, he began to mutter, to breathe out an inaudible monologue, to discuss with some unseen auditor how he would do this, would do that, how he would set about repairing the canvas.

After a while Mrs Invach wandered away and left him to it, and began again her own endless search for lost things.

Wee Robin

This story was told me by my aunt Martha. When she was younger, Aunt Martha used to pay regular visits to a rich friend, the Countess of Stoke, who had been a schoolfellow of my aunt some years before. The Countess now lived in a big old house, Tyle Place, which her husband's family had owned for hundreds of years. The house had twelve bathrooms, my aunt used to tell me, wide-eyed, and on her visits she was always given a room with a bathroom of her own. This was luxury and splendour for Aunt Martha, who, at home, was used to share a bathroom with her five sisters.

But one year she found herself quartered in a different bedroom with a different bathroom, and her hostess said to her, "We are so sorry about this change, Martha, dear, but the pipes are leaking in the room that we generally give you, so we had to make the change. But still, we hope that you will be comfortable." My aunt said that she was sure she would be; the new room seemed very pleasant, and the bathroom that went with it was even bigger than the one she was accustomed to.

"There is just one thing," said the Countess, "one little thing I should mention. It is best if you don't *sing* in the bathroom."

My aunt wondered a little what could be the reason for this, but was too polite to ask. Perhaps, she thought, the partition walls were very thin—for two bathrooms had been portioned off, long ago, from one bedroom; perhaps next door there might be quartered some other guest with highly sensitive nerves who could not abide the sound of singing; some simple reason of that sort there must certainly be. At any rate, whatever the cause, she readily promised not to raise her voice in the bathroom.

A great number of other guests were staying at Tyle Place that year, for it was the Christmas season; there were young folks and older ones, there was present-giving and playacting, games and dancing; day followed happy day and Aunt Martha seldom sought her chamber until well past midnight, when she was too tired to do anything but seek her bed as quickly as might be. But when she did retire she always remembered her friend's prohibition and never, when she was within her own domain, made the mistake of raising her voice in song.

But one night toward the end of her visit the younger guests had been gaily country-dancing in the huge old raftered hall which was the most ancient part of Tyle Place. Fiddlers and pipers had been sum-moned from Tyle village, and most of the party had been dancing until well into the small hours. Then the tired players were handsomely fee'd by the Earl and Countess, they took their leave, and the young guests started upstairs to bed, some of them, at least, still wishful to remain downstairs a while longer and go on dancing. Through the closed front door they could still hear the village band gaily playing their way down the hill. The tune they played was "Gathering Peascods," which, as it happened, had been the final dance before the party came to an end. My aunt Martha heard the music come floating through her bedroom window, which faced forward on to the approach drive.

Without thinking, Martha began to whistle—for she had a clear and tuneful whistle, like a boy or a blackbird—and, still without think-ing, in her happy mood after the festivities, she plucked her nightgown off the bed, where it was laid out for her, and danced her way into the bathroom still whistling "Gathering Peascods." A joyous, lively tune.

What was her astonishment, then, to see a wee boy sitting on the bath mat by the bath, naked as a bullrush, and crying his heart out!

"Who in the wide world are you?" says my aunt Martha.

But he cries all the harder and makes no reply.

Well, Aunt Martha could not bear to see him so cold and shivering—for it was a bitterly cold, frosty December night—so she puts round him her own woollen bed jacket and wraps him in a quilt on her bed.

"Who are you?" she says again.

But all the answer he gulps out through his sobs is: "I want my Mammy! I want my Daddy! I want Nurse Ellen!"

Well, Aunt Martha is as puzzled at this as may be, for, to her knowledge, none of the other guests had brought a child with them to Tyle Place. But she says:

"Wait a little minute, my dearie. I'll fetch your Auntie Delia and she'll soon have ye sorted."

Then she runs along the passageway and down the stairs, to where her host and hostess are still discussing the end of the party.

"Delia, come quick!" she calls. "There's a wee boy in my room, and, poor little dear, he seems clean moithered! Not a stitch on him and calling for his mammy!" Poor Countess Delia turns white as a pillow-slip.

"Oh my dear!" she says. "Just what I hoped would *not* happen!"

"But who is the poor child? And who are his parents? Come to him, quick, quick!"

"I'll come, my dear, but the chances are he'll not be there . . ."

Sure enough, when they return to Martha's room, there's no sign of the child; the jacket and quilt are there, snugged round on the bed as Martha had left them, but the wee boy was gone.

"Where can he be?" cries Aunt Martha, and runs into the bathroom. But the child is not there either and—what strikes Martha for the first time—the bathmat he had sat on was gone, too; but there was still a plain blue woollen mat hanging on the warm towel rail.

"We'll never know where he has gone," says the Countess.

"But who is he? And who are his parents?"

"Dead and gone, my love, these hundred years. That's the pity of it."

"What can you mean, Delia? And who is the little lad?"

"He's Wee Robin."

So the Countess tells his story.

"He had a godmother, Lady Astoria Vane, who was the cousin of his father, the Fourth Earl. Lady Astoria doated on the boy. She was a great traveller, as ladies were at that time—this was early in the nineteenth century—she went to Turkey and the Lebanon, she visited Ceylon and Cashmere and many Arab lands. And from these places she used to send back lavish presents to her godson, many of which he was too small to appreciate. The line of silver elephants on the side table in the dining room, for instance, and the stuffed camel in the conservatory. And, when he was four, she sent him a magic bath mat."

"A magic bathmat!"

"Such an unsuitable gift for a four-year-old! Of course nobody knew that it was enchanted. They did think, however, that it was too handsome for a child. Well, you probably saw it. It was Chinese silk, wonderfully woven and embroidered."

Now Aunt Martha remembered that she had been faintly surprised to notice that there were two bathmats, one of plain wool hanging on the warm rail, and the one on which the boy sat, glossy with colour and brilliantly embroidered.

"The fourth Earl, Robin's father, was a very talented musician. He played many different instruments, and he composed music as well. He often used to play tunes to the little boy, who, like his father, loved music. He was always humming and singing—in his bath, in his cot, when he walked out in the park. And—it is thought—one of the tunes that he hummed or sang must have activated the magic mat, which they had put in the bathroom. There was a nursery maid, Ellen Rigby—she walked into the bathroom one evening, ready to give Wee Robin his bath—there he was, sitting on the mat, humming a tune, happy as a sandhopper—and then—the next minute—there he was not! Clean vanished. They searched, of course, they called, they hunted—first the whole house, then the gardens and park, then the village. They told the police. They advertised, locally and in national newspapers. None of it was any use. They never saw Wee Robin again. Both parents died of grief. They had no other children. So the Fourth Earl's cousin inherited the house and land and the title."

"But why has he come back now? And why didn't he stay?"

"Hearing a tune sometimes fetches him back—from whereever he has gone—no very happy place, it seems; he always seems very forlorn and bewildered."

"Have you seen him, Delia?"

"Once. And Charles has seen him once."

"Poor, poor little creature, I do wonder where he comes from."

"And where he goes back to. Perhaps it is a different place every time. He is still hunting for his parents. And for Nurse Ellen. There is a belief among the local people that, if you see him three times, he will stay with you. But no one has ever seen him three times."

Secretly, Aunt Martha resolved to try and see Wee Robin again. His sadness, his loneliness, his strange plight had touched her deeply. The Countess offered to change her bedroom for the last three days of her visit, but she said no to that.

And every time she went into her bathroom she sang or whistled "Gathering Peascods." Once, she had a fleeting glimpse of Wee Robin, skinny and forlorn, sitting on his mat.

"Oh, won't you come with me?" pleaded my aunt Martha. "I'd look after you—I'd love you—I'd teach you and care for you and make a home for you—!" But all he whimpers out is "I want my Mammy! I want my Daddy! I want Nurse Ellen!"

Gone, all of them, long into the past.

And before Aunt Martha could touch or soothe or persuade him, he was gone again, back, perhaps, to where he had come from. Or to some other desolate corner of time or space.

My aunt Martha never married. Never had a child of her own. I think she always hoped that she would see Wee Robin a third time. But her friends left Tyle Place and it was pulled down. A wind farm occupies the site. Forty great spinners stand there, whirling their arms against the sky, and if Wee Robin comes visiting there, he must find it bleak indeed.

The Fluttering Thing

A line of men trailed wearily across the plain. They made slow progress, shuffling along, one behind the other. Red beams from the setting sun cast their shadows sideways off the embanked track and across the quaking bog which lay on either side of it.

The men did not speak to each other; they stumbled along in silence. Each of them was thinking about food. One dreamed of lamb stew, another of a cheeseburger, another of crab salad. They knew they would get none of these things when they reached the end of their march. The evening meal would be grey gruel, as it had been at breakfast.

Their minds on food, the marching men kept their eyes on their feet. They did not look ahead or sideways. They had come this way so often that there was nothing new to fix their attention. Beyond the bog, and all around them, lay a ring of smouldering volcanoes. Each one belched out pink or grey smoke. Now and then they spat up a fan of sparks. From time to time a trickle of molten lava slid down the side of one of the mountains. The marching men ignored these occurrences, which were nothing new.

Now and then a man would fall to the ground, unable to walk any farther. He would be ignored by his companions. Perhaps, after a few minutes' rest, he might struggle to his feet and recommence walking. Perhaps not.

At the rear of the column were guards with machine pistols. These were seldom used. If the fallen man appeared to be dead, there was no need to shoot him. His body would be tossed into the bog, where it instantly sank from view. If he proved to be alive, and able to go on, he would be prodded to his feet.

If alive, but too weak to walk, he went into the bog.

A man called Mark was talking to himself as he plodded along. He was in the middle of the column, with half his companions ahead, half behind him.

He was not talking aloud, but inside his mind.

"Moist sugar, raisins, currants, candied peel, flour, salt, nutmeg, cinnamon, eggs, milk, grated lemon peel, brandy. Some say grated carrot. Some say mashed potato. I say no. Some say mace. Boil for six hours, or steam for at least seven. Serve with a suitable sauce, perhaps brandy butter. Did I say flour? Did I say salt? Heat a tablespoonful of brandy in a spoon over a candle, set light to it, and pour over the pudding before serving. Mashed potato! What a revolting suggestion!"

At this moment the man called Mark saw something unusual just ahead.

A live creature was floundering in the bog on the left-hand side of the causeway. Something was in difficulties there. Due to the coating of black mud it was impossible to decide whether it was human or animal. Neither would last long before sinking out of sight.

Most of the trudging men had passed by without taking the slightest interest in what was taking place by the side of the road. If they thought about it at all they assumed that it was one of their companions who wished to put an end to his dismal existence.

But Mark, for some reason, decided differently. He strode out of the moving column, knelt down, extended a hand, grabbed the nearest part of the creature that he could reach, and pulled hard.

The rest of the marching men paid no heed to this attempt at rescue. They plodded on their way.

Mark pulled again—tugged—twisted.

With a loud, sucking gulp, the bog released its victim. The black, slimy body suddenly exploded out of its gluey socket and landed on the bank, knocking Mark off his feet.

"I thank you!—I thank you!" gasped the stranger as Mark scrambled up and was about to resume his plodding march. "Wait! Don't go! I am able to reward you! I have a—I have a—a thing."

"Errrch. A—a thing?" Mark was so much out of the habit of talking that his words came out in a thick croak. "A thing?" he said again.

"A magic thing. A wish thing."

The muddy stranger pulled a kerchief from his pocket and, crouching at the roadside, carefully wiped an object that he had been clutching in his right hand. It was about the size of a hen's egg.

"Found it—on the volcano—Mount Tlextac—" gasped the rescued man. "My great-grandmother—told me—about them—"

"Which volcano?"

"Tlextac. On the first day of autumn—or the last day of spring—the fire mountain throws up these pods—"

"Pods? Looks like a stone to me."

"No. There is something inside. Something alive."

"Alive?"

"Yes. But you must never let it out. Or the power is lost."

"*Power?*"

"Power to grant a wish. One wish every twenty-four hours. Anything you want. A wish to each person who holds it—I was just going to wish," the muddy man said, "when the mountain heaved up its crust and threw me into the bog. If it weren't for you, I would have sunk. So now I am going to wish my wish, and then I will give you the pod—don't open it, whatever you do, or the power will be dispersed—"

The muddy man stretched out his muddy hand and laid the curiously heavy oval object in Mark's palm.

"Saints! I can feel something fluttering inside—like a chick inside an egg—horrible!"

"Yes, but *whatever* you do, don't let it out—or no more wishes."

The stranger drew a deep, croaking breath. Then he laid a finger on the object in Mark's palm. He said, "I want to go *there!*" and immediately vanished. But the heavy, egg-shaped stone remained in Mark's hand. The fluttering inside it was now frantic. It tickled, it shivered, it struggled.

"Poor devil in there," thought Mark. "What can it be? What it must be like, trapped, shut up inside that hard, heavy case—"

He studied the solid, egg-shaped object.

It was greenish grey in colour, slightly shiny where the stranger had rubbed it with his handkerchief. A thin white line ran round its widest circumference. "Can that be a crack?" wondered Mark. "Like the opening of a box. I wonder if it unscrews . . . ?"

"Come on you—number ninety-four!" called one of the armed guards. "Get going!"

He prodded Mark with his pistol. Mark took a couple of steps forward.

He said, "I want a Christmas pudding!"—and then sharply unscrewed the object with a twist of both hands. The two halves separated smoothly. There was nothing inside, apart from a drop or two of greenish fluid.

Mark heard—but did not see—something that whisked up into the air above his head and immediately fluttered away over the bog towards the distant mountains.

Mark threw away the two halves of the pod and stooped to pick up a Christmas pudding which lay in a dish at his feet on the muddy ground. Somebody had just poured flaming brandy over it.

"Hand that over!" said the guard.

Water of Youth

Gay and glorious, one day every year, the market square of this little town is, and that's the day in September when the fair comes, and music peals, and roundabouts whirl, and the through-traffic, if it wants to get by, has to give the town a miss and scrape along side lanes past sodden blackberry hedges. Though where through-traffic should be going, don't ask me, for beyond the town, up the mountain, stands nothing but the water tower, on its one leg like a broody heron, and the castle of Owen Richards the poet; beyond again, and all round for that matter, lie only the mountains, heaving their mossy shoulders into the rain and the mist.

On Fair Day, then, the big roundabout takes up all the centre of the town square with its horses and swans and dragons, while round it thick as currants in a birthday cake crowd the sideshows and stalls and rifle-galleries, not to mention Jones the Rope Trick, the lovely fortune-telling Myfanwy, and, this year we are speaking of, Señor Pedro.

Señor Pedro was a wizened little man, nose like a parrot, eyes like chips of anthracite, hair a mere wisp at the back of his head, and a walnut shell face that was wrinkled and seamed all over as if, every night, he slept facedown on a doormat.

Indeed, he was talking about his face, standing on a big box in front of his little tent. The box was wreathed about with pink paper, and on the tent hung a banner: *Agua de Vida, Water of Life.*

"You see my face, señores, señoras?" he was shouting to the crowd. "Wrinkled, you think, my friends, but you are wrong. My face was scratched by thorns, yes, thorns—those very thorns that the South American pygmies use to tip their arrows. On the slopes of the Andes, your honours, grows a terrible thorn thicket, many miles across. In the middle of this thicket is a spring. Ah, your honours, such a beautiful spring! Nowhere in the world is there one like it—this is the spring of the water of youth. One sip removes twenty, thirty years from your age."

"A fine story to tell us, that is!" shouted a derisive voice. "Why hasn't anyone ever heard of this water before?"

Shrugged a patient shoulder, Señor Pedro did. "Am I not telling you, señoras, señores? This water is very hard to procure. The Indians are hostile, the place is distant, the thicket is impenetrable and peril-ous, *muy periculoso.*"

"If the water does that to you, why don't the Indians drink it and stay young forever?"

"*Quien sabe?* Maybe they do. Who can tell what age a pygmy has reached? But what I am come to tell you, señoras, is that with me I have"—here he brought it from under his jacket and held it up with a flourish—"a bottle, the last bottle in Europe, of this renowned, mirac-ulous, youth-giving liquid brought to you all the way from Brazil." There was a murmur of wonder from the crowd, and they gazed at the stone bottle, which was crowned with gold foil and might hold a quart.

"Why don't you drink it yourself?" shrilled Mrs Griffith the Dis-pensary. "Poison I believe it is!"

"Ah, there's probable! Or why should he be offering it for sale when he's as worn and wizened himself as an old seed potato?"

"Maybe he prefers the money, fair play?" suggested Rhys the Red Dragon.

"Why should I wish to grow younger?" said Señor Pedro scorn-fully. "One life with its troubles is enough for me. I have all I need.

Back in the Andes my good wife is waiting for me, beautiful as an angel. But the dearest longing of her heart is a new grand piano, for though we stood the legs of her Otway in four pans of kerosene, the termites ate it away until nothing remained but the keys."

"Did you ever hear of such a calamity?" mourned the sympathetic crowd.

"Her only wish is to play once more. And that is why, señoras, señores, at risk to my life I filled six bottles with the water of youth and came to Europe. Here you see the last of them. I am now going to auction it. Will any gracious lady or gentleman offer me five hundred pounds for it, this miraculous elixir, this water of youth?"

"Come on, now, Lily Griffith! Tickled to death your old man would be, to see you a lovely young twenty-one-year-old again!"

"As if I'd waste my money on such stuff," sniffed Mrs Griffith. "Better things I have to do with it. Five hundred pounds indeed!"

The crowd hesitated, broke, laughed, and chaffered. Señor Pedro kept the auction bubbling like a lukewarm kettle.

There were other attractions in the square. Music thundered between the houses, there were goldfish to be won by a skilful fling of a dart, hot dogs to be eaten, vases and tea sets at the rifle gallery, candy floss for the children; and all the time the rain pelted down. But the great shafts of light pushing upwards from the sideshows turned the rain to a canopy of sparkle.

Owen Richards the poet came down from his castle to the fair with Ariel, his guest, a famous actress from the boards of London, and the love of his long life.

"I must have my fortune told," said she, making a beeline for Myfanwy's van with its sugar-pink stripes and the portrait of Myfanwy over the door which had so bewitched Ianto Evans two years before that he had gone into the van and never been seen again.

"You at least should have no worries about your fortune, Ariel," said Owen, but she shuddered as she glanced into a little shell-encrusted looking-glass that he had won at the rifle gallery and caught a glimpse of her lovely, ageing face. He followed her into the sugar-striped van.

Myfanwy was playing waterfalls with a pack of cards which she could pour from one hand to another like water from a cup to a can.

"Tell my fortune," commanded Ariel, and she put out her hand.

"Steady you must hold it, then," Myfanwy bade her, and she built a card-house on Ariel's palm, ten, jack, queen, king, and the ace for a roof; Ariel neither budged nor spoke.

"Second storey is it," Myfanwy said at that, and she built another on top of the first. Ariel held her hand steady as a table—a fine, thin hand, and the wrist so transparent you could see the veins in it. "Fancy now," Myfanwy said, and she laid a third storey on top of the second. "Very unusual that is."

But still the tower stood without falling on Ariel's palm, and Myfanwy pursed her lips and added the final storey, four black spades and the ace on top of it all.

"Now blow," she said, and Ariel blew, scattering the cards like a shower of apple-blossom across the tent. Myfanwy picked them up. A look of amazement came over her face.

"O dammo," says she, "crazy old fortune you've got here. Neither head nor tail can I make of it! Try again, you must."

"No, I'll not try again," says Ariel, laughing. "I'm not wishful to tempt Providence too far. We'll leave it at that." And she crossed Myfanwy's hand with a flourish of half-crowns.

"Can't you say if she'll marry?" asked Owen Richards the poet, anxious as a hen with one duckling.

"Far as I can make out she'll have more husbands than Henry the Eighth," Myfanwy says. "A heron must have flown over the van and bewitched the cards. Good luck to you, lady, and remember Myfanwy in your will."

Ariel laughed. "Maybe I'll never make a will," she said. Out they went into the rain again.

Soon as they were gone, Ianto Evans, he that had left his good wife for Myfanwy's sake two years before, crept out from under the bed. "Ten o'clock," he said. "Blodwen will have been out to Jones the Cod to buy her bit of fish and chips. Locked away snug, she'll be, watching the telly; I'll just nip along home and dig up the clematis by the back door. Planted that clematis myself, I did; no reason it shouldn't come with us on our wanderings. Lovely little flowers it has, like red butterflies."

"Careful now, Ianto, bach," Myfanwy said. "Supposing she's out at the fair? Meet her you might, and then the fur would fly."

"Not Blodwen, not her. She never went to a fair since the day she was old enough to pop a penny into a moneybox." And off he strode into the silvery wet night, and sniffing up the alley to his back door like a hound on a fish trail—only he was on the track of Blodwen and her Friday four-pennorth, to make sure was she safely locked up with the hake and chips. Smell of fish there was, sure enough, but it had been left by Thomas the Electric, four houses farther on. Just put the clematis in his pocket, Ianto had, when Blodwen came along with her supper and let out a screech at sight of him.

"Oh, there's my skulking husband that ran off and left me for a cardsharping Jezebel! Wait till I get my hands on you, Ianto my man!"

Ran he did, like a hare, and she after him, down the alley, through the coconut shies, into the square, past the learned pig, between the tenpins, up the skiffle alley, and three times round the hot cat stand. Towards Myfanwy's van he fled, meaning perhaps to hide behind her skirts, and then, gaining a bit of sense before it was too late, turned aside into Jones the Rope Trick's enclosure.

"Save me, Jones man, save me!" he bawled.

The crowd cheered and laughed, for most of them had felt the weight of Blodwen's tongue at one time or another, and they were on the side of the underdog. Quick as a wink Jones picked up his clarinet and tootled out "Men of Harlech." The coiled rope stood up and begged like a hamadryad; no monkey ever climbed quicker than Ianto shinned up it hand over hand.

When Blodwen arrived, ten quick seconds later by Morgan the Turf's stopwatch, he was out of sight into the black wet sky above.

"Gone he has, ma'am," says Jones, very sober. "Angels are singing 'Cwm Rhondda' round him this minute, likely as not."

Blodwen gave Jones one look, one, but enough to loosen every stopping in his teeth, and then she turned on her heel and started for home; she knew when she was beaten. But on her way, having lost her hake and chips in the chase, she stopped at the stand for a hamburger and tomato sauce.

Meanwhile Señor Pedro had sold his water of youth to Ariel the actress for two hundred and seventy pounds, nine shillings and ninepence. "Only to such a lovely lady as you would I part with my precious water for so mean a sum," he mourned, handing over the gold-wrapped bottle.

"There's crazy for you!" said Mrs Griffith. "Fancy spending all that good money on an old bottle with like as not nothing but tap water inside it."

"Try a drop!" shouted the crowd.

"Throw it away!" begged Owen Richards the poet. "Marry me, Ariel! Forget about the moribund old theatre, is it? Stay here! Queen of the whole town you'd be."

But Ariel looked about at the crowd, and in her voice that could sing or whisper its way up to the tiptop seat in the gallery, she called, "Who can lend me a corkscrew?"

Morgan the Turf had his whipped out a photo finish ahead of Rhys the Red Dragon, took the bottle, and opened it with a bow.

Set her lips to it, then, Ariel did, and a quick swallow with her. Then she stopped, half laughing, half scared, crying, "Dare I go on?"

"Throw it away, Ariel love," Owen Richards begged. But the crowd shouted, "Drink up, ma'am!"

Now a law of physics there is, see, very unbreakable, which says, "All that goes up must come down." And just at that moment what should come down but Ianto Evans like an old blockbuster plump into the middle of things. Knocked the bottle clean out of Ariel's hand he did—lucky she'd put the cork back—and himself pretty near silly.

Soon on his feet again he was though, for when Blodwen, teeth halfway through her hamburger, loitering to enjoy a free spectacle for once in her cheeseparing life, laid eyes on him, she was after him again like an old pike after a springtime salmon, and off into the dark alleys he fled, clasping the bottle in his frantic hand. Once he tripped and fell and dropped it; Blodwen swooped on him, but it was the bottle she grabbed in her haste, not Ianto.

"Oh, but I'll have you yet," shouted the termagant, and while Morgan the Turf was going round laying two to one on Blodwen, the pair of them kept it up round the town, ding-dong, now here, now there.

No lie, now, for many a long year after, if a man wanted to describe something faster than mere speed he'd say, "Like Blodwen Evans the night she was after her husband, Ianto."

Meanwhile, what of Ariel? you will be asking, and indeed to goodness there was wonder enough in the way the years were dropping off her like layers of gauze. No more than nineteen she looked now, as she stood scared and smiling, and a long ah! at her beauty trembled through the crowd. Only Owen Richards in grief turned his head away; he knew she was lost to him forever now.

"Oh! "she cried, "I'm afraid, I'm afraid of what is happening to me! Must it all begin again, the doubts and terrors of youth? Comfort me, Owen dear, tell me I haven't changed. Owen, comfort me!"

But he in silence held up to her the little shell-bordered looking-glass. When she had looked once it seemed as if the weight of her beauty would crush her like a snowfall in May. Stepped away, she did, hanging her head, and the crowd parted in a hush as she walked to her car.

"Back to London, is it?" said Owen, standing with his hand on the bonnet.

"Back to London, indeed," said she, sighing.

"Then good-bye, my love."

Her tears splashed on the steering wheel like raindrops as she drove away to face her new legend of life and the harshness of being young. Owen, with a heart of lead, turned back, but with no spirit in him for the fair.

"Let's hope we've seen the last of that bottle; unsettling it is," Rhys the Red Dragon commented.

And Mrs Griffith said, "Indeed to goodness, yes!"

But Blodwen, now: breathless, with tomato sauce sticking in her gullet like china clay, she had stopped the chase of Ianto a moment to take a swig at the bottle, hoping maybe—knowing her Ianto—that it would be whisky. But no more than a couple of good gollops had she taken ("Ach y fi, it's only water, then!") when she laid eyes on Ianto stealing back to Myfanwy's van behind the big roundabout.

Quick as a weasel after him, Blodwen. Over the roundabout she went, threading her way between horses and swans. "Give us a break, Alun, man!" shouts Ianto. "Start her up, then!" And Alun threw in his gears with a thrashing like an old whale in convulsions. Slow at first, then faster, spinning in a giddy gold spiral, switchbacking up and down, round went the swans and dragons, a whole glittering stableland of bucking broncos.

Well! stuck fast Blodwen was, and had to make the best of it, clinging tight to a swan's neck. But the bottle, spun out of her hand by another natural wonder known as centrifugal force, flew off like a bullet over the heads of the crowd, and nobody's eye followed it into the dark.

Gone, and a good riddance too, Owen Richards thought.

Back to his castle then, poor Mr Richards, to live out his final years with owls and ink, in an everlasting third act of spiderwebs. Or so he thought.

Sitting over a bottle of claret he was, late enough for tomorrow's moon, when half the town came tapping at his door, timid but trustful, for to whom but a poet can you turn when life throws up such a problem as the roundabout had tossed them?

"See here, Mr Richards, bach, an orphan we have on our hands," says Morgan the Turf, very solemn, and the crowd shoves forward a small girl, blackhaired, sapling-thin, fierce as a fury.

"You're the wisest man in this town, Mr Richards, dear," the neighbours said. "Fitting it is you should have charge of this child of misfortune. Too young she is to live in her own house alone, see; and her husband run off with the fortune-teller."

"Husband?" said Owen Richards, and then he looked closer and recognised Blodwen Evans of forty years ago—Blodwen Pugh as she was then.

Tears of rage there were still on her cheeks, but forgetfulness had followed her plunge back into childhood. Her anger had left her, and she gazed at him with no more than wonder for an old poet and his cobwebbed castle.

"Live with me, is it, my dear?" said Owen.

And she in awe answered, "Yes, sir," and bobbed a curtsy. Nodding approval, the town fathers withdrew to the Red Dragon.

Where, all this time, you will be asking, where is Señor Pedro, the author of these troubles?

Not a man to outstay his welcome, the little pedlar, and he was tramping out of town down the rainswept highroad with his two hundred and seventy pounds when a speeding pink van overtook him.

"Lift to Cardiff?" called a head from the window—Ianto's.

"I thank you; yes."

"Wet old night it is for walking," Ianto said as the little man unslung his pack and shook the mud out of his turn-ups.

"Indeed, yes."

"No more of those bottles, have you?" Ianto asked, handing over a mug of tea and a hospitable wedge of cake as Myfanwy drove them on their swift way.

Señor Pedro shook his head.

"Just as well then," Ianto said. "More trouble in that bottle than in a whole keg of whisky, if you will be asking my opinion."

"You do not think that to grow younger is a blessing?"

"Not for Myfanwy and me." And Ianto looked fondly at the back of Myfanwy's neck as she bent over the wheel. "All we wish is that we grow old together and die on the same day."

"Ah," Señor Pedro said with sympathy, and he thought of his own dear wife on the slopes of the Andes.

What became of the bottle? you will be wondering, and the answer to that is easy: it fell into the town reservoir, standing on its one leg farther up the mountainside.

Put up the water-rates like a shot, the council would have, had they guessed, but nobody did; though, as the years went by, and no one in the place grew a day older, people did begin to wonder why. But in a town the folk get used to one another's faces, and nobody thought about it very deeply as they went about their business. Visitors might have wondered at it indeed; become a famous tourist centre, the place might have, but for the seeds in Pedro's turn-ups.

Scattered some of those famous thorn seeds he had—whether by mistake or on purpose, who can say?—and almost overnight a dense thicket of brambles sprang up that soon had the town surrounded. Nobody noticed; too wrapped up in their own concerns they were, with council meetings and oratorios, weddings, and Gorsedds, all pre-sided over by Owen the poet and his happy adopted daughter, Blod-wen; Wales will hear of her, too, one day, indeed, if copies of her poems ever find their way past the thorn thicket.

So there you have them: Ariel still a lovely legend on the boards of London town; Ianto and his Myfanwy, old and wrinkled and gay as two crickets travelling the country in their fortune-telling van, with the flowers of the clematis—its roots safely bedded in a pickle-pot—fluttering like red butterflies over the roof; Señor Pedro long since back with his piano on the slopes of the Andes; the townspeople living their carefree unchanging lives till the Day of Judgment.

And what have any of them done to deserve it?

Not a thing.

No moral to this story, you will be saying, and I am afraid it is true.

Acknowledgments

On Joan's behalf I would like to thank all her faithful readers and supporters. Special thanks must go to Gavin J. Grant and Kelly Link of Small Beer Press for their ongoing commitment to publishing Joan's work. I would also like to thank author, editor, and science fiction expert John Clute for his dedicated work in creating a bibliography of Joan's five hundred–plus short stories, which has been an invaluable resource, and his encouragement for this project. Finally, love and enormous gratitude go to Charles Schlessiger, agent now to three generations of Aikens, for his tireless devotion and enthusiasm, courtesy, and expertise.

—*Lizza Aiken*

Publication History

These stories were originally published as follows:
"A Mermaid Too Many," *Argosy*, November 1957
"Model Wife," *Argosy*, July 1956
"Girl in a Whirl" (as by Nicholas Dee), *Argosy*, May 1957
"Red-Hot Favourite" (as by Nicholas Dee), *Argosy*, March 1958
"Spur of the Moment," *Argosy*, January 1959
"Octopi in the Sky," *Argosy*, December 1959
"Honeymaroon," *Argosy*, September 1960
"The Sale of Midsummer," *Ghostly Grim and Gruesome*, Helen Hoke, ed., 1976
"The Helper," *A Touch of Chill*, Gollancz, 1979
"Introduction" and "The Monkey's Wedding," *Night Terrors*, Lois Duncan, ed., 1996
"Wee Robin," *Silent Night*, Holly Street, ed., 2002
"Water of Youth" (as "Come to the Fair"), *Argosy*, September 1961
"The Fluttering Thing" (2002), "Second Thoughts"(1955), "Hair" (ca. 1955),
"Harp Music" (1960), "The Paper Queen" (1960), "Reading in Bed" (ca. 1955), and
"The Magnesia Tree" (1960), appear here for the first time.

Joan Aiken (1924–2004) was born in Rye, Sussex, England, into a literary family: her father was the poet and writer Conrad Aiken and her siblings the novelists Jane Aiken Hodge and John Aiken. After her parents' divorce, her mother married the popular English writer Martin Armstrong.

Aiken began writing at the age of five, and her first collection of stories, *All You've Ever Wanted* (which included the first Armitage family stories, which were all gathered in a posthumous collection *The Serial Garden*), was published in 1953. After her first husband's death, Aiken supported her family by copyediting at *Argosy* and working at an advertising agency before turning full time to writing fiction. She went on to write for *Vogue, Good Housekeeping, Vanity Fair, Women's Own,* and many other magazines.

She wrote over a hundred books and was perhaps best known for the dozen novels in *The Wolves of Willoughby Chase* series. She received the Guardian and Edgar Allan Poe awards for fiction, and in 1999 she was awarded an MBE.